Are There

Horses in Heaven?

Based on a true story

Mary Lou Davis

CHRISTIAN
FOCUS

Mary Lou Davis is the co-author of *Flight Path: A Biography of Frank Baker Jr* (ISBN 978-1-85792-918-8) and author of *The Truth that Transformed Me* (ISBN 978-1-84550-206-5). *Horses in Heaven* is her first young adult novel. She also writes for magazines and public radio and is a widely published photographer. She and her husband and three children are adventure addicts. They all enjoy rock climbing, water skiing and racing mountain bikes. Although she grew up riding and showing horses, she traded in her living, breathing mount for one of metal and rubber. She now rides a CRF 250 motorcycle on tracks and through the woods of Alabama.

Copyright © 2007 Mary Lou Davis.

ISBN: 978-1-84550-283-6

10 9 8 7 6 5 4 3 2 1

Published in 2007
by
Christian Focus Publications Ltd,
Geanies House, Fearn, Tain, Ross-shire,
IV20 1TW, Scotland, Great Britain.
www.christianfocus.com

Cover design by Moose77.com
Printed by CPD, Wales

Contents

Acknowledgements

In his classic novel, War and Peace, Leo Tolstoy wrote, "Mother knew how to win my passionate devotion simply by drawing out what was best in my soul and admiring it." I echo his eloquent words about my mother, Janie Buck. I would not be the person I am today without her drawing out the best in me. She not only taught me to love God and walk with him, she drew me into her writing projects and encouraged me to fly on my own. She admired my efforts in everything I did and nurtured the bud of creativity until it blossomed. Also, father's unconditional love has been a visual representation on earth of God's heavenly love for me. Thank you Mom and Dad, Bill and Janie Buck, for making me the person I am today.

Anita Cowart was my other mother who put up with me through adolescence at the barn. She has been the true inspiration for this story. I am grieved that she never saw this story as a book because of her untimely death. She was an amazing artist who painted not only with accuracy, but something else I can only describe as a spark of love and grace. She also was a wonderful writer. Her own book about Love, though unpublished, has been photocopied and passed around the world. Her memory will be remembered with love and honored by all who knew her. The following is one of the last things she wrote.

"Life on the farm was hard in the winter. Often water pipes froze and we would have to haul water from the river in garbage cans in the back of the truck. It seemed so futile as much of it would splash out as the truck lurched over the frozen road on its way back to the barn, but it would be so nice to sit by the fire and warm our icy fingers. Life went on and we knew spring was coming! Soon the dead black limbs of the trees would burst forth in flowering glory, rejoicing that the night of winter was over. The mares would drop their hairy coats for sleek and shiny ones of spring. Little colts and calves would pop up everywhere.

As we walked the long distance from the barn back to the house on many a cold winter's night we could see the lights beckoning in the distant windows of our beautiful house. No matter how long and hard and cold the day, there was hope in our hearts for the house held warmth, nourishment, and rest. It was a promise to me that at the end of the winter of old age here on earth that we will see the lights of our heavenly home beckoning to us. At the end of every winter season in our lives, there is spring, or home, or the resurrection and finally entering our eternal home and the fulfillment of all the promises of God."

Big Man

*A*race seemed like a good idea at the time, but as I felt the muscles of my horse stretch and contract in full gallop, I realized we'd made a mistake.

Jericho's mane lashed my face as I leaned forward to grab the reins that dangled uselessly from the bit clenched between his teeth. The leather lines whipped against his churning legs and danced wildly away from my grasp. "I'm such an idiot," I hissed through clenched teeth. How could I have dropped the reins? "Whoa! Whoa!" I yelled and lunged for them again. I had to stop him.

Jericho's staccato hoofbeats echoed the pulse pounding in my ears. Through nostrils, wide and red, he sucked air in and out in a noisy cadence that matched the beat of my heart. Sweat foamed a white lather that slimed my cheek and seeped into the corner of my eye as I lay flat on his neck. The salt stung and I blinked to clear my vision. But, I didn't need to see what lay ahead; I knew with certainty what was coming. Above the clacking hooves and blowing horse I could hear the music of tires whining along asphalt. The highway!

"Jump; Mary!" Katy yelled. Her mount couldn't come close to matching Jericho's long stride. On her short-legged pony she ran behind me uselessly shouting dumb instructions like, "Grab the reins!"

What did she think I was trying to do? Pick my nose?

"I knew I would die young," I whispered to the wind. "This is it."

It's true. Your life does flash through your mind before you die.

As a baby my first words were, "I want a horse." And I never stopped repeating the phrase until my wish was granted.

If the government sponsored a research project to analyze brainwaves of little girls, I'm sure it would find that visions of horses occupy 95 percent of their gray matter. I'm not sure if every child in the world is obsessed with horses, or only every girl in my elementary school.

My friends and I spent hours on the playground speaking to one another in a high-pitched falsetto.

"Lightning, let's go to the pasture to eat grass."

"Neeyyy, neeyyyy!" Lightning would answer and a pack of little girls would gallop away looking somewhat like

King Arthur and his knights in *Monty Python's Holy Grail*, except without coconuts to clack together.

I think Monty Python got the idea for their movie when he saw a little girl's whinnying and cantering around teeter-totters.

My heart's desire was finally realized in the fourth grade.

It had been a traumatic year. My last name was synonymous with fear among boys my age. When the words, "There's that Buck girl," echoed across the playground they scattered in terror. My best friend, Katy Pickle, and I took particular pleasure in biting our nails till they were sharp and ragged. We'd chase down the boys baring our lethal claws like hungry tigresses out for a kill. Each scratch inflicted was a trophy. We kept tally marks to determine who scored the most.

One of our favorite fellows to torment was Bill Sanderson. He was cherubic with a halo of golden curls and rosy cheeks. But his portly stature and short legs made him an easy catch. I would grab his legs and drop-tackle him while Katy shoved pea gravel down his pants. He'd howl and cry, but all the other boys were too terrified of "that Buck girl" to come to his rescue.

I don't recall any adults ever scolding us. I'm not even sure there was recess supervision. All the teachers were apparently on coffee breaks or taking naps. The playground was a mighty free-for-all with Katy and me wreaking havoc and terrorizing the boys with our jagged fingernails.

But then it happened. Everything changed and my life would never be the same. It wasn't gradual. It happened all at once as if a wound-up rubber band snapped and like the Grinch my heart grew three sizes in a moment.

As usual, Katy and I had chased down Bill. We had him down, and as I pushed my fingers into his hair to grind his face in the dirt he flipped over and looked at me with those wide tear-filled baby blues. Sweaty blonde curls framed his pudgy cheeks and I hesitated. If only I hadn't, my life could have been so different. But I did.

I paused and in that brief lull the world slowed down.

The kids on the playground froze.

All noise and chatter ceased.

The wind stopped whipping us into a frenzy.

My heart backflipped and the thought came unbidden into my mind, *Hey, he's kind of cute.*

Just as suddenly the world started whirling again. Kids screamed and ran and everything flew by as if nothing had happened.

I rocked back on my heels and stared at Bill. He couldn't believe his luck and began crab-crawling backward as soon as I released my grip on him.

"Why'd you let him go?" Katy asked staring at me as if I'd lost my mind.

"Why do birds suddenly appear every time he is near?" I sung under my breath.

"What are you mumbling about birds for?" Katy said, and put her hand to my forehead as if I had a fever.

"Just like me they long to be, close to you," I sang and spun in a circle.

The next day I sealed my fate. I wore a dress and began a diary.

Young girls' diaries record their secret innermost longings, which mostly boil down to vapid lines on their latest infatuations. Usually a flap with a metal latch and a lock secures the book from prying eyes.

I soon wished I had this kind of protection for my soul's yearnings. Mine were recorded in the back of a school notebook – easy prey for prying eyes. I called it my deery. Who knows why? In it I chronicled my sudden crush on Bill Sanderson.

The flowery poetic lines revealed a side I hid, for fear it would ruin my reputation as Attila the Hun. In a lapse of judgment, or possibly a desire to be better friends with LuAnne Holcomb, I bared my soul. I showed her my deery.

Two minutes later she ran and narked on me to Bill. I guess, in hindsight, I can hardly blame her. It was the greatest scoop in our elementary school history.

The treachery was committed while I, unsuspecting, was in the girl's bathroom. In those few moments spent washing my hands my status changed from top dog on the playground to the dirt under the pea gravel.

With his new status of beast of prey, Bill lay in wait outside the girl's bathroom door. When I walked out I stared through his beady blue orbs into his dark soul; I knew in my gut the name, "that Buck girl," held no more terror for him.

The grinning face of LuAnne Holcomb quickly dispelled any doubts I may have had. But a quick step in her direction sent her cowering behind Bill in a ready-to-run posture.

For the rest of the year I was tormented by a new song, "Deery, deery, Mary has a deery," conducted by a strutting Bill Sanderson. The tune, recognized by children worldwide, usually accompanies the clever lyrics, "Ne, neh, neh, neh, neh."

Bill became quite adept at "Mary has a deery." He even made up a dance to go along with the tune. He wagged his behind rhythmically back and forth like a fat dog hoping for a bone, and swung his arms in wide counterclockwise circles. It became a popular dance and caught on all over the United States and Canada. In fact I saw them line dancing the "Mary has a deery" on *Soul Train* a few months later.

The rest of the year I sat near the door at recess and kept my eyes on the ground, sifting pea gravel through my fingers.

My parents must have guessed something was amiss since I went from a boisterous tomboy to a timid female overnight. When we got news that the high school football coach's house burned down and he had a horse to get rid of, Dad thought the time had come to heed my deepest longings. Hence "Big Man" joined the Buck family.

Big Man was a big old bay – brown coat with black mane and tail. I never knew his pedigree, but he looked part thoroughbred, part draft horse. He was a kind, old giant and patient with a scrappy little hellion like me.

I could ride pretty well already. I cut my teeth on horses during the summers and on holidays at my grandmother's farm in L.A. That's Lower Alabama to the uninitiated. With bridles held together by discarded hay string, my cousins and I guided our mounts down white sandy trails that wound through the Conecuh National Forest.

Summers were so hot the tar on the roads became molten. It sucked the bottom of our sneakers with a slup, slurp as we walked across the asphalt – that is if we were lucky enough to be wearing sneakers. Mostly we went barefooted and fried the skin off our feet.

We'd swim the horses in Open Pond or Blue Lake for relief. However, when a man got his arm twisted off and swallowed by a gator, we gave Open Pond a wide berth.

Big Man was a horse of many talents. He could stretch his long, black upper lip straight out like a charmed snake rising for a kiss. If you pulled straight up on the reins of his hackamore, a bridle that stopped the horse by means of suffocation rather than a steel bit in the mouth, he'd rear up on his hind legs. He'd pose a moment, for a snapshot, then plop back down looking bored as if you hadn't just shouted, "High ho, Silver, away!" I could slide down his tail – without fear of being cannoned to the moon – crawl under his belly and ride him backward while cantering.

He was the perfect first horse, except for the fact that he was about 100 years old and couldn't keep the pace of a nine-year-old hyperactive child. This is why I found myself flying toward the highway on the back of a half-broke three year old named Jericho. My mind snapped back to the imminent danger I faced.

"Jump!" Katy yelled again.

I gave one more futile attempt to catch the dangling reins and stop the speeding locomotive.

A car flashed by ahead.

The highway!

I leapt sideways screaming bloody murder. I'd like to say the world stood still a moment and I saw everything clearly for a brief second, but I'd be lying. In less than the blink of an eye I landed in honeysuckle vines woven through prickly blackberry bushes that lined the side of the road. I cartwheeled and tumbled knowing every bone in my body, including my neck, was snapping in several places.

"You Okay?" Katy asked as she pulled her horse up beside me and jumped off to survey the damage.

Honk! Screeeeech! I jerked up on my elbows and watched Jericho thread the needle through speeding cars. A cloud of smoke boiled behind a station wagon as it lay a line of rubber on the road in an effort to keep from plowing over the big bay gelding. With ears glued flat back on his head he ran the gauntlet without slowing.

Clackety, clackety, clack, his hooves rang like hammers nailing the asphalt. He wove through the traffic then soared over the fence into the pastures of Heathermoor Farm.

Heathermoor. Take a deep breath and say it again. Can you smell the fresh-cut grass and the horsey scent that fills the space between the letters? The word, Heathermoor, is enough to stop me for a moment of reverential silence. It was my second home – a horse farm. It's located off Highway 119 – the old Indian trail that runs through a narrow fertile valley of rolling pasture land. On either side of this valley, mountain ranges rise like sentinels standing guard over the land below. Well, a Colorado cowboy might call them big hills, but to Southerners they're mountains.

A quarter mile of white board fence lined the front pastures of Heathermoor. They framed the green fields, sprinkled through with grazing mares and foals, like living works of art. A long paved drive led to the brick and board house set like a jewel at the crest of the hill. White paint chipped off the brick giving it the cool shabby-chic look before the word shabby-chic was ever coined. Giant elms stretched wide arms protectively over it.

It was a place of wonder, dreams and heartbreak.

At Heathermoor the Cowart family raised and trained American Saddlebred show horses and a passel of other kids along with their own children. Mr Cowart was strong and thick, his wife small and thin.

Mr Cowart's face, weathered and brown like saddle leather, was crinkled with laugh lines. Everyday he wore his uniform – khaki pants and a white button-down shirt. Even in the heat of summer he always looked as though he were headed for the office instead of the barn.

He loved to tease us, correcting our grammar like a schoolteacher. "Where's it at?" he'd mock with his salt and pepper eyebrows shooting up to the hayloft. "What kind of language is that? Never end a sentence with a preposition. Don't they teach English in school anymore?" Or he'd say, "What fur? What fur? Cat fur to make kitten britches. It's, what for, not what fur. You sound like white trash talking like that. And I'll tell you what for, because I said so!"

When he'd pick us up and threaten to dunk us in the garbage can full of water in the hallway of the barn, Mrs Cowart would shriek, "John! Stop tormenting those girls!" She couldn't stand physical violence and Mr Cowart's wrestling made her nervous.

She was our second mother, treating us with all the kindness of one who can hand a child back to the real mom for discipline. She took every opportunity to show us God's love and his works in everyday situations.

Mrs Cowart always wore a line of concern between her eyes. As a child I had no idea of the depth of the tragedy she had experienced or the pressures involved in running a horse farm on a shoestring budget. I didn't give any thought to the imminent dangers that come with mixing horses with children, but I'd soon find out.

Horse Fever

K aty and I loved to sit with Mrs Cowart on the back porch in summer or in the den by the roaring fire in winter. She told marvelous tales about her life and the miracles that happened on the farm.

"From the time I saw mules plod past our house when I was a little girl," Mrs Cowart said, and closed her eyes remembering, "I was enslaved."

We were sitting in the cool shade of the back porch glad to be out of the heat that blazed in shimmering waves on the rolling fields beyond the fence. Our horses tethered by bridle reins switched flies with their tails as they stood in the shade of the elms.

"By the time I was six," she continued, "I had identified the fluttering and murmurings deep within me at the sight or smell of anything equine. They were early symptoms of "horse fever."

"Daddy was stationed at Pearl Harbor during World War II and our family moved to California to be closer to him. To take my mind off the war Mother bought me my first horse. His name was Sox. I trained him to jump, count by pawing the ground with his hoof and nod his head to say yes. On my command he could lie down or stand on his hind legs.

"After the war, before we moved back to Alabama, Mother said I had to sell him." Mrs Cowart laughed her funny laugh — a cross between a giggle and a snort. "I thought if he didn't sell I could bring him home. So every time somebody came to see him I'd wave my arms in a signal for him to rear up. Even though he never sold, I still didn't get to take him with me." Mrs Cowart sighed and gazed into the distance as if she could still see him in her mind's eye.

We loved to hear about when she and Mr Cowart had been in college together. She took her beloved horse, Madame, to the University of Alabama.

At age nineteen Mr Cowart purchased a black horse named Mike with money he got by selling his blood to the Red Cross. He would ride Mike over the manicured lawns and across the sidewalks of the University.

It was very romantic. He, a knight on his steed, would ride to the art school to pick her up after classes. They'd ride double across the Quadrangle dodging mustangs and cougars — that is Ford Mustangs and Mercury Cougars. The cars honked and waved at the four-legged oddity that waited at red lights beside them.

After they married, Mr Cowart joined the paratroopers and they were forced to sell their small herd. When they christened their first son, Mike, everyone thought he was named after the horse. Love and Richard followed their big brother in quick succession and it looked like owning horses was history.

"That is," Mrs Cowart laughed, "until High Finance came along." She pointed in the direction of a swaybacked, arthritic horse who stood morosely in the field. High Finance was now out to pasture enjoying the fruits of retirement.

Mrs Cowart's sister, Brownie Evans, had wanted a horse. The Evans and Cowarts pooled their money, even searching under sofa cushions for spare change. After raising the enormous sum of $175 they named their new acquisition High Finance.

But they soon grew tired of sharing Finance between their two families. The Cowarts found another horse that lived in a car repair garage. Its stable mates were old tires and broken trucks. The horse was part Saddlebred, and Mrs Cowart said she wanted him more than anything. They had spent their fortune on Finance and didn't have a large enough sum to buy the new horse.

One night Mr and Mrs Cowart had a brainstorm session.

"Nita, you could set up your own lemonade stand," Mr Cowart suggested with a grin.

She laughed, "There's already enough competition in this neighborhood with the girls' stand on our side of the street and the boys' on the other. Each side slashes prices and sweetens the deal to win customers. The girls promise to sing and dance and the boys pretend to be injured to lure folks to stop."

"Really, John," she sobered. "Isn't there something we can sell so we can buy that horse?"

They studied the living room furniture. "Mother would kill me if I sold any of my furniture, china or silver. She's dead set on me turning out to be a 'Mt Brook lady' like she is."

"It's too late for that don't you think?" Mr Cowart snickered, "I like you just the way you are."

"Like?" she asked, watching him from the corner of her eye.

"You know I love you, but I think it's more important that I like to be with you too," he said, kissing her tenderly on the forehead. He jerked her back, gripping her arms with wide eyes and a big grin.

"Hey! I know what we can sell! That old stove your mother gave us. It's just sitting in our basement."

The next day Mr Cowart loaded the stove in the back of a company truck and went out to bargain with the owner of the horse. Before he even knocked, the door opened a crack and moonlight gilded the long barrel of a shotgun. It pointed straight at Mr Cowart's head.

"I'm unarmed," Mr Cowart shouted. He held his perspiring palms up in plain sight. "All I've got is a stove!" he called.

The gun barrel lowered and the man's head poked out. He surveyed Mr Cowart with squinting eyes, "I knew that," he grumbled. But before he walked out he glanced right and left in case someone was hiding in the bushes.

They made an even trade – the horse for the stove.

Soon afterward the Cowarts sold their Mountain Brook home and bought a five-acre farm off Rocky Ridge Road.

It was on that five-acre farm the Cowart's love affair with breeding and showing horses blossomed. "Horse lovers such as I are incurable," Mrs Cowart told Katy and me. "Many are snared by the fun of riding, the sport of showing, or the art of breeding. But after many hours and dollars under the equine spell, fancy or circumstances often pull their attention elsewhere. For the 'congenital' kind of horse people, as we are, something equine is as necessary for well-being as healthy eating habits or good digestion."

Katy and I heartily concurred. We wanted to be just like her. Horses were part of our genetic composition too. When on vacation, I'd get withdrawals and have to find a horse so I could bury my nose in its neck and inhale. I was like an addict who gets trembly without a fix. A snort of horse scent helped quell the tremors.

As the Cowarts' stock began to multiply, their five-acre farm became overcrowded.

"Nita," Mr Cowart said, "let's make this business work."

Mrs Cowart had never seen her husband so excited. "What do you mean, John?"

He smiled his crooked grin, raised one eyebrow and whispered, "I think we can turn the horses into a financial asset instead of a burden. All we need is a bigger farm."

"John! You've got to be kidding. We've barely paid for this place. We don't have the money for a big farm." Mrs Cowart loved the little farm. With the few horses they had she could practically wrap her arms around them all at once. But Mr Cowart kept persisting until she caught the virus. "If you think we're meant to move to a bigger place, let's ask God."

There was nothing else they could do. They didn't have money for that kind of venture so they prayed, "Lord, give us a story whose very facts prove that you do exist and act in the lives of modern men like you did in Bible days. You said if we delighted in you you would give us the desires of our hearts. If your will is for us to pursue this business, give us a farm."

Two weeks later God showed up. Mr Cowart's employer called him into his office one day. "John, I've got something to talk to you about." He sat behind his desk and began shuffling papers.

Whenever a boss begins a conversation like that most people begin to sweat. The first question that pops into their mind is, "What'd I do now?"

Mr Cowart stood nervously shifting from foot to foot, waiting for Mr Bodkin to continue.

Finally, Mr Bodkin found what he was looking for and cleared his throat, "John..."

He paused to put on his reading glasses, "I've made a decision."

"A decision," Mr Cowart repeated. What was coming, promotion or demotion?

"But, there's a problem," Mr Bodkin continued, taking his glasses off again and wiping the sweat from his forehead with the back of his hand.

"A problem," Mr Cowart repeated.

"Yes, that's what I said," Mr Bodkin gave Mr Cowart a level look, "I've decided to make a large investment, but I'm at a loss as to how to see to it."

"An investment," Mr Cowart repeated.

"Yes, that's what I said," Mr Bodkin replaced the reading glasses on his nose and looked over their rims at Mr Cowart. "Would you and your wife be interested in looking after it for me?" he asked, as if that explained everything.

"Looking after it?" Mr Cowart repeated.

"Do you have to repeat everything I say?" He slammed the papers down. "I know it's asking a lot. If you're not interested I'll understand." Again he removed his glasses and placed them on top of the papers.

"I'm not sure if I follow you," Mr Cowart said.

"Don't you have livestock?" Mr Bodkin asked. "I've heard you talking about your horses."

"Yes, sir. We've some nice Saddlebreds and a couple of two year olds my son is working with."

"Well, that's why I thought you'd be interested in taking care of my investment."

"You want to invest in our horses?" Mr Cowart stepped forward with excitement. He hoped to get some interest in the colts but had no idea Mr Bodkin was a horseman.

"No! I want you to move them to my new investment – a farm I bought near Leeds. It's 120 acres with a five-bedroom house. There's no way I can take care of something of that magnitude. I need to find someone who will live there and care for it till the land appreciates in value. Ever since I decided to buy it, I just couldn't get you off my mind. I thought I'd run it by you. There'd be no rent, but you'd pay for the upkeep."

Overwhelmed, Mr Cowart was struck dumb. He stood opening and closing his mouth several times like a fish out of water. Finally he answered hoarsely, repeating, "Move in to your investment?"

When I first began riding at Heathermoor I dragged Katy along with me. The Cowarts always managed to scrounge up a horse for her to ride. Before long Katy and I had become permanent fixtures at the farm.

From the very beginning I had a love affair with the Cowarts and would have legally changed my name if possible. We called Mrs Cowart Ma and Mr Cowart Pa. Looking back, I wonder if it hurt my parents to see me push them away and cling instead to the Cowarts.

The Cowarts had three children in two and a half years – Mike, Richard and Love. Exhausted and finished with child-bearing, Mrs Cowart laughed when her children ganged up on her and began to pray for another brother. You know what they say about childlike faith. Peter followed two years later.

Junior horse-trainer from a tender age, Mike, the oldest, broke colts, trained them to show and won blue ribbons. He named his prize pony Snowfire's Memory. Mrs Cowart always wondered what the memory was.

The farm was a child magnet. Mike was ringleader of all the stray kids the Cowarts attracted. They would skip around in a circle pretending to ride magnificent show horses with him as judge. After the performance everyone lined up and listened for Mike to call out the winner. Fist-fights ensued to contest the places he awarded.

Other kids followed baseball players' batting averages. Mike knew every horse's pedigree back to the Civil War. Mrs

Cowart once heard him reciting to a visitor, "This one's great, great grandfather carried General John Hunt Morgan, leader of the Rebel guerrillas, Morgan's Raiders."

For every Southerner it all goes back to the Civil War. That is, "the War between the States," there was nothing civil about it.

At horse shows when the organist played our National Anthem – Dixie – everyone in the crowd would stand, hand on heart, and sing with gusto. "I wish I was in Dixie, Away, away. In Dixie land I'll take my stand to live and die in Dixie... Look away! Look away! Look away! Dixie land."

I always wondered why they wanted me to avert my eyes. Look away from what?

Richard, the second son, rode the horses with a loose style all his own. At the tender age of six he began riding in shows. At a canter one of the horse's front legs leads or goes ahead of the other. In a competition the rider signals his mount to lead with the inside leg. When the judge called "Canter," Richard would lean over to check if he was on the right lead. A collective gasp would ripple through the crowd as if everyone was certain the little blonde boy was about to tumble off and break his neck. Unaware of his precarious position, he'd wobble upright again and finish the class in perfect harmony with the horse.

When Richard turned thirteen the Cowarts had a gelding no one could ride. The horse launched Mr Cowart so high the bridle ripped off at the apex of his flight. Mrs Cowart broke her ankle when it unseated her. Richard, like Alec of *The Black Stallion*, was the only person this horse let on his back.

They gave up on breaking the horse to carry other people besides their thirteen year old, and took the wild beast to the horse sale in Atlanta. They contemplated writing in the sale bill, "Even a thirteen year old boy can ride him," but decided that would be unethical. Someone might get killed. Finally, they listed the horse as "green, broken only to lunge."

The next year they saw it listed in the *Saddle Horse Review* as a "promising new fine harness horse." Someone else must have learned the hard way not to try to ride him since he was relegated to pulling buggies.

At six years old their daughter, Love, wanted a white horse. Mrs Cowart found one advertised "cheap" and went to investigate.

"Here's the darling," the oversized owner crooned as she walked around the side of a rickety corrugated tin shed. Behind it a chain link fence enclosed a small yard containing a pig, some chickens and the white horse.

"That'll be $75." The large woman held out a pudgy hand.

"I'd like to see it move before I pay you." Mrs Cowart eyed the reclining figure with suspicion. It lay immobile and was impossible to determine with the naked eye if it was breathing.

The woman clucked her tongue and patted the chain link fence. Ching, ching, ching, the fence rattled. "Here Silver. Come on to momma darlin'."

Silver didn't bat an eye.

"Is it alive?" Mrs Cowart asked.

The woman chuckled nervously then squeezed her bulk through the gate. She waded through the mud, her pink house shoes slurping through the muck.

She grabbed hold of the horse's halter and began a tug of war. "Come-ooof-on-uuggghhh-Dar-ooff-lin'!" she huffed with every jerk. For a moment it looked as if the horse would stand. The head lifted and legs trembled then straightened. But gravity won and the animal didn't budge. The fat lady didn't sing, but Mrs Cowart knew it was over.

Deciding to get Love a horse she would be proud of, and take to shows, Santa Claus tied a little pop-eyed welsh mare to a tree outside her window on Christmas. Love christened her bay pony "My, My" after the great world's champion of that time. But her everyday name was Madame in honor of the old mare from her mother's childhood

Peter, the baby the older children had prayed into existence, grew up with a wild hair. Mrs Cowart admits she was too tired to discipline him as consistently as she had his three older siblings. He was the male counterpart of the child in the nursery rhyme about the girl with the curl in the middle of her forehead. When he was good he was very, very good, but when he was bad he was horrid.

Otis, the old black man who helped the Cowarts on the farm, took Peter fishing when he was little. Upon delivering him back to Mrs Cowart he motioned to Peter with his chin, "Dis un's gonna be trouble. I can tell by de way he walks."

Otis wasn't a prophet or the son of a prophet, but his prediction was money. And as a teenager Peter was the heart-throb of every girl who crossed his path.

At the time I began riding at Heathermoor, the Cowart's children were older and not around the house much so Katy and I decided to fill their empty nest.

The farm was the perfect baby-sitting service for our parents. We were dropped off early and picked up late. The hours in-between were filled with all kinds of danger and ad-venture. Katy and I lived to imitate everything the Cowart's daughter, Love, and her best friend, Franny, ever did.

Franny bounded into Love's life at the age of five. Before the Cowarts moved to their farm they lived across from Mt Brook elementary school. An hour after the moving truck left, their doorbell chimed. Upon opening the door, Mrs Cowart thought someone had pulled a prank.

No one was there.

Hearing a loud "Ahem," she looked down and saw a pretty, golden-haired child with a very confident face. The cherub demanded, "I want to see the little girl of the house." Ever since that day Love and Franny were inseparable.

Franny had a sense of adventure big enough for both girls – it was big enough for a whole neighborhood of girls. Confined to the two of them, it exploded into hair-raising feats, some of which they barely survived.

At five years old, Franny suggested they build a fire in the basement ventilator to smoke out the cat. With gray clouds billowing along the base of the house, they were happily adding fuel to the flames when the maid discovered them.

"Laudy, Laudy! Chil', what are you up to? Yo' mamma gonna take a switch to yo' legs!" She snatched the juvenile delinquents by their elbows and began screaming, "Help! Somebody put out dat fire!"

Volunteers were rounded up from the neighboring houses to fight the blaze.

Bold and fearless Franny, the youngest of four kids, would take on anybody – children, animals, even grown-ups. At six she climbed a ladder that leaned against a neighbor's house. The woman knew the tiny hooves dancing on her roof weren't reindeer. Upon finding a child cavorting up there, she called, "Come down here this instant before you fall and hurt yourself."

Arms akimbo, Franny faced her belligerently, "Aw, you're not worried about me, you're just worried about your dumb ol' roof."

Love was the opposite in temperament – quiet, studious and reserved. The combination of their personalities at polar extremes seemed to hold the two in balance.

If imitation is the highest form of flattery, Katy and I paid generous tributes to Franny and Love. For when we heard their stories of daring deeds we did our best to copy everything they did.

Angels Under Bridges

*T*here was something magical about Heather-moor Farm. The wind carried wonderful scents – fresh-air, new-mown grass and wildflowers – mingled with horse sweat, manure and sweet feed. It was a potpourri I wish I could bottle and take with me everywhere. It said, "You're at the barn."

Everything was technicolor. The trees greener and the sky bluer as you stepped from the sheltering elms in the yard onto the yellow dirt road that led to the barn. It was like entering Oz. Katy and I explored every square inch.

Two front pastures flanked the house. The pasture on the left had a small pond called the keyhole. It wasn't much more than a big ditch when it was dry, but we rode through it taking depth charts. If it hadn't rained too much you could ride across it on a tall horse without the water coming over the withers.

But in the rainy season the little spring-fed pond overflowed half of the pasture. We'd canter bareback through the knee-deep water singing commercial jingles such as "Coke adds life," and other tunes from the radio as the water splashed around us from our horses' pounding hooves. It diffused into thousands of drops around us and caught the light like tiny diamonds that cast rainbows in the mist. I always dreamed some talent scout would drive by on Highway 119, see us, and sign us up for the next nationwide cola commercial.

When the Cowart boys were younger they would go fishing in the puddles. Mrs Cowart chuckled when she saw them. But as an artist she admired her children's vivid imagination that they could catch something in a puddle. Then one day Richard brought in a string of bream, vindicating his effort. After another flood, a neighboring farmer picked up forty fish that were flopping in the shallow puddles! "They ride in on an underground river," he said, grinning toothlessly at her shocked expression.

As a teenager Peter brought two of his harem to the farm. To impress them he hitched DC Battle, the standard-bred racehorse who never forgot the track, to their homemade roadster buggy. The little carts that roadster horses pull are called bikes. They have a single seat where the rider sits. His feet perch in metal cups beside the poles that run up either side of the horse and are attached to the harness. The cart Peter drove was one that Mr Cowart had welded together from scrap metal. Its long bench seat between two beefed-up bicycle wheels was wide enough for two people.

Peter squeezed between the girls who wrapped their arms around him and giggled. But as the three took off on the two-seater bench for a romantic drive something went wrong. DC Battle forgot where he was. He must have heard the far-away echo of the trumpets blaring the start of a race. In his mind he was back at Belmont track. He took the bit firmly between his teeth and began to fly around the front pasture. Peter stood, like Ben Hur in a chariot race, and sawed on the reins with all his might to stop the wild ride. The girls, faces distorted by the "G" forces, shrieked and clutched the sides of the careening chariot.

In desperation to stop before they were all killed, Peter leaned on the left rein with all his might. This maneuver turned the rampaging horse straight into the keyhole pond. DC Battle dove in, hardly slowing. The cart emerged on the other side carrying three bronzed statues. They were completely covered with muck. Mr Cowart made Peter walk DC the rest of the afternoon to cool him down.

The pasture on the right had a larger pond that was fed by a wet-weather stream. In a drought it would dry up almost completely; but in the spring and early summer it was good for swimming. Highway 119 passed over a bridge at the edge of the property forming a concrete tunnel the creek passed through. Although we tried often enough, it was all but impossible to make the horses wade through that echoing cavern. It was spooky under the shadows of the bridge and the tangle of brush and trees. The wind whispered through the foliage and we wondered if there was something the horses could see that we couldn't. We had heard that animals see things humans can't ... like ghosts ... or even angels. There was after all that story about the car and the bridge....

At one time, a car had careened off the bridge and crashed into the creek on the other side of the road. For several days the driver was missing. No one knew what had happened to him. Finally, someone spotted the car and he was rescued. He had been severely injured and was unable to free himself from the wreck. He told his rescuers that angels were with him the whole time he had been down in the creek.

I believed in angels. I was saved in that very spot years later by what had to have been an angel.

The house, anchored on a rise between the pastures, had been a show place featured on the glossy pages of *Home and Garden* magazine. The right pasture had once been graced by a garden with a pump-fed waterfall that flowed through an apple orchard and down to the lake.

In the spring the fragrant pink clouds that covered the crab-apple, cherry and peach trees accented the white blooms of the pear. To the right of the house was a formal garden bordered by boxwood. A brick-lined path led you into its center. It must have been a wonder at one time.

Mrs Cowart told us that Love spent a lot of time there and cherished it as her own secret garden. Katy and I always whispered when we ventured into its ruins as if we walked on hallowed ground.

A large arbor covered with muscadine grapes flanked one side of it. Katy had never eaten muscadines so I demonstrated. "First, you pick one off." I chose a large purplish one. "See? There's a little hole where it came off the vine, if not, nip a slit in it." I took a tiny bite out of the top. "Squirt the innards into your mouth, and thet the theeds outh, lithe thith," I said, separating the seeds from the fruit. It was a tricky process requiring teeth, tongue and lots of grimacing.

"Pttt. Spit out the seeds then," gulp, "...swallow." I held up the outside peel of the grape. "You don't want to eat this. Its thick as saddle leather."

I gathered several more. Katy selected a green one. "No!" I yelled, making her jump. "It's got to be kind of purple, or it'll be too sour. Try this one." I handed her one of the choice ones I had just picked.

Tentatively, she bit the top off and squirted the fruit in her mouth. She tried to separate the seeds with her tongue but grimaced then spat several times, unsuccessfully. She wiped her chin with the back of her hand and looked with distaste at the mushy grape entrails at her feet.

"Nasty!" she spat again, then wiped her tongue with her T-shirt. "It's a lugy, like you spit when you're sick. See, its even green. Gross!"

"You're sick!" I said. "It does not. It's good – it's putting the South in your mouth." I sucked up several more, but she walked away shuddering.

"You're just a Yankee!" I yelled after her. That was as good as a cuss word. She turned around with her fists raised. "Am not! Take it back."

"Only a Yankee wouldn't like muscadines. My grandmother told me so." It was a lie, but it sounded good. We settled it with a wrestle under the arbor. I pinned her down and twisted her arm. "Say I'm a Yankee."

"You're a Yankee!" she shouted.

"No! Say *you're* a Yankee!" I twisted harder.

"I did!" She squealed, "You're a Yankee."

"Say, Katy Suzanne Pickle is a Yankee," I applied even more pressure.

"Mary Lou Buck is a dang Yankee," she yelled. Her voice echoed off the lake and came back faintly, "Yankee, Yankee."

She kicked me in the back and sent me sprawling. Eventually we made up and walked back to the center of the garden.

The brick walk circled what must have been an old fountain. It was empty. Weeds grew through large cracks that jigsawed its bottom. Katy and I closed our eyes and imagined what it had looked like in its prime – fountain splashing, roses scenting the area with sweet perfume and Love communing with the Lord.

Behind the house the white fence ran along the back-yard and lined the middle pasture. A dirt road cut the green turf in half. It tunneled beneath huge overhanging live oaks. At the terminus of the road was the barn. It had the classic lines of old barns in coffee-table books. Painted white, its red doors were always open as if to say, "Come on in, ya'll." In the shade of the hallway flies congregated, too savvy to be taken in by the bug zapper a conscientious parent had hung from the rafters. Its blue lights hummed uselessly overhead.

In the summer the whir of fans in each stall greeted you as you entered, making the barn sound sleepy and feel cool. Cross ties, ropes with hooks, hung in the hall. Show horses were brought out from the stalls, clipped into the cross ties and readied for workouts.

At first Katy and I paid little attention to the show horses except to be awed by their beauty. There was so much ground to explore on the farm and trails in the mountains surrounding it. But unlike Alexander the Great, who sat down and cried after conquering the world, we had more to set our sights on after we had conquered the surrounding territory.

In the main pasture the Cowart boys had made a moto-cross track where they rode their Combat Wombats, Hadaka Super Rats and other motorcycles with macho monikers. My brother, Billy, brought out his Super Rat dirt bike to race with them. Back then there was no such thing as chest protectors, knee guards, or elbow guards. The daredevils were lucky if they even had motorcycle helmets. They held one race at the farm where several of the riders wore football helmets.

The guys took great joy in getting a girl on the backs of their bikes. They'd lure them with promises. "I'll go slow. You can trust me." Then they'd go screaming around the motocross track, the gullible girl clinging to their back like a wet washrag. Peter, after much coaxing, got his mother to get on with him. He immediately wheelied down the fence line with her shrieking, "Peeettterrr!" That was the last time she ever threw a leg over one of those machines.

Katy and I would run our horses over the track when motorcycles weren't out. It was fun galloping up the jumps and feeling the weightlessness of the drop on the other side.

We mostly rode bareback, which was great in the winter, because the warmth of the horse was like sitting on your own personal radiator. But in summer the friction between girl and beast would create a lather of sweat and hair that soaked our jeans and turned them white. Often it was so hot we wore shorts. When we'd dismount, the horsehair would stick to us. We'd look like creatures from Narnia with a girl's body and a goat's legs.

The Little Cahaba River ran behind the barn creating a natural boundary for the back pasture. Cahaba was an Indian name meaning River of Life, or Waters from Above. There's an old prophecy that said when the Big Cahaba flooded God would come down. If that is true about the Little Cahaba, God visited often.

When it flooded, the creek would rise ten feet or more. It flowed so high the concrete bridge that spanned it would disappear completely under the rush of muddy current.

It may have been during one of these floods that God visited Love. In her journal she wrote that God revealed an awesome secret to her. I wondered if she heard him speak or was it just an impression? However he revealed it, she was sure it was God speaking. And what he said came true.

When the Little Cahaba wasn't flooded the water ran eight to ten feet below the bridge. There was a small rapid with a shallow pool above the rocks where we girls swam.

My parents told me to stay out of the Little Cahaba because it was polluted. I think they said it after I had been swimming there for several years. I must have developed a tolerance for whatever bacteria was in it because I never turned green or glowed in the dark, or whatever pollution is supposed to do to you.

After the river left Heathermoor property the Little Cahaba meandered over to Mr Pool's land where it formed a secluded swimming hole. The trees sheltered a deep spot where they bent their branches low and dangled their long fingers in its slow current.

Mr Cowart said that Mr Pool bought cotton, which was a polite way to say he didn't work much. I never saw Mr Pool in anything but overalls. It was a wonder how he perpetually had gray stubble on his face but never a beard. He kept cows and goats and lived in a shack from the previous century. An open hall called a dogtrot separated its two rooms and a shed stood out back with a half moon cut over the door making us wonder if they had indoor plumbing.

Mr Pool and his sister sat on their front porch all day. I suppose for entertainment they'd watch the kittens play. With no TV they'd never seen the *Brady Bunch*, or *Candid Camera*, and didn't care if they ever did.

We felt as if we'd stepped back in time when we rode onto his land. It amazed Katy and me that in modern society any one actually lived in a place like that. But Mr Pool was kind and let us have free reign of his land. He always welcomed us when we'd ride into his goat pasture. "Just don't chase dem cows," he'd warn. Which was kind of like asking the fox not to chase the hens.

Those fat old cows looked up with big doe eyes as if to say, "Neh, neh, neh, neh. You can't catch me!"

They were right too, our saddle horses rounded corners as well as a semi-truck, so we never could cut the cows out like real cowboys and soon lost interest.

Mr Pool always knew when we'd given in to the urge to play cowboy. "It'll make the milk sour if you chase them jerseys." His T's sounded like D's because he'd lost most of his teeth. His lips sunk in where teeth should have been, except for the bulge that betrayed the wad of snuff. I wondered how he knew we'd chased the cows. They were a long way from his shack. It must have been telepathy.

Lady Godiva

Katy and I developed a habit of carrying wire cutters. It was a trick I picked up riding with Franny.

"If there's not a way, make one," Franny quoted Hannibal (the one who rode elephants over the alps not the scary guy from the movies). "Your best friend is a set of wire cutters in your back pocket," she said patting the pocket of her Levi's from which the handles of the tool protruded. "Love and I could get our ponies to crawl through the wire fences. We'd hold the top wire up and the bottom wire down, and Madame and Boogaloo would crawl through after us. But with a big horse," she gestured at Jericho, the seal bay gelding I rode, "you have to make a gate."

Franny demonstrated by cutting a "gate" in the fence of the back pasture. She made a loop in the wire to hook it back after we went through. Forging a way through trees and brush, we emerged on Rex Lake

Road. It was quieter than Highway 119 and a short cut to the Jitney Junior store. Since she was six years older, Franny had ready money. Because she was my brother's girlfriend she lavished me with candy as if I were her little sister.

Rex Lake Road ran right past Leeds Country Club. The golf course's manicured rolling fairways always tempted me to run across the greens. The Club sparked memories for Franny of the times she and Love sneaked out at night after her parents were asleep.

"The Cowarts used to pack Madame up in the horse trailer and deliver her and Love to my house for the weekend." She sat backward on Boogaloo to face me and launched into a story.

Franny lived on a sort of compound in the center of Mt Brook. A large Georgian mansion stood at the end of the long drive. Behind it was a swimming pool, kennels, tennis courts and a small stable. It was its own resort. Franny's family was well known in Alabama. They even had a whole county named after them.

"Krispy Kreme is open twenty-four hours," she grinned. "So Love and I would creep downstairs after Mom and Dad were asleep and sneak out. We'd ride Madame and Boogaloo through the woods and neighbors' yards down to Mountain Brook Country Club.

"Boogaloo always left his calling card on one of the greens. I'm sure the green-keepers had duck-fits wondering where in the world those giant turds came from." She laughed. "It was good fertilizer."

She took a deep breath and sighed. "Its exhilarating to ride in the cool night air – a tremendous sense of freedom. The moon was our only light with a sprinkling of stars.

"Everything looks different at midnight in the city. Shadows danced under the streetlights and played games on our imagination.

"Love constantly looked over her shoulder when the leaves crunched under our ponies' hooves. When headlights announced a car coming, we'd dash behind a house or take off cantering, jumping low hedges in yards to get away. We thought a cop might catch us and call my folks.

"Oh!" she sighed, smacking her lips, "There's nothing like hot doughnuts – especially Krispy Kremes." The first time we showed up on the ponies the whole night shift at Krispy Kreme came out to pet them. They even gave us free food. But after that we had to bring our own cash.

"Eastwood Mall is right across the street. During the day we'd ride over and get money for pony tricks. We were our own wild west show." Her eyes flashed and I visualized her as Calamity Jane.

"One time we didn't just ride *to* the mall, we rode *through* it." She dabbed the laughter tears with her shirttail. "I talked Love into holding open the door for me, and reluctantly, she followed."

"We cantered up the long hall between the stores. I called like a hawker at the State Fair sideshow, 'Pay a quarter; see the horse buck.' Love went along with it, although she didn't say a word. She just held out her baseball cap and collected quarters."

Franny flipped her legs around, facing front on Boogaloo. "Did you know she bucks on command?" She laid her hand on Boogaloo's rump close to her pony's tail. Immediately, as if an invisible string jerked from the sky, Boogaloo's bottom shot in the air, tail swishing and back legs kicking. Franny sat the buck with ease, looking for all the world like a female centaur. I was impressed.

"We made a good bit that day," she recalled. "That is before the mall manager chased us out. But we got enough to cross the street and pick up a dozen hot ones at Krispy Kreme before heading home."

Long before Katy or I started riding at Heathermoor, Love and Franny had cut a "gate" in the rusting wire of Mr Pool's fence. Taking a short cut through it seemed better than riding out to the road and passing by the house at the entrance of Mr Pool's land.

Those people in that house scared us. They had junk piled everywhere. An old car without an engine, TV's with no guts, a dead refrigerator, boxes, trash, broken toys, you name it and it was piled up in a heap around the house and yard. It felt kind of creepy to ride by, so we always took the wire cut "gate" to Mr Pool's.

One hot day Katy and I rode to the swimming hole in the Little Cahaba at the back of Mr Pool's land. We rode straight into the water on the horses, stood on their backs and disrobed. Katy, who was meticulous, folded her clothing, placing it neatly on her mare's rear. I stuffed mine through the top of my horse's bridle. In the sticky humidity of the South wet clothes don't dry, and you run the risk of getting diaper rash by sitting around in wet underpants. However, that wasn't the only reason we forsook clothing. It was fun to skinny-dip just for the sake of feeling the cold water on areas of our bodies that never get the opportunity to feel it in polite company.

"Cannon Ball!" I yelled jumping off my horse's rump. The current carried me downriver where I grabbed the trailing reins to keep from being swept too far downstream. Katy jumped from her horse's back to mine and grabbed one of the hanging branches. "Aaeeeaaaeeaa," she Tarzan yelled and swung before dropping in.

At first the horses were content to act as jungle gyms. After awhile, Katy's mare decided it wasn't fair for the humans to have all the fun and decided to take a dip herself. She began pawing and grunting, which is the first signal that your horse is going to roll. She shivered all over like a dog shaking the water from its coat.

I think that's when it happened, although I can't say for sure. Neither one of us saw until it was too late. If we had seen it we might have saved them, but alas, they disappeared under the muddy water and were never seen again. At least that's my version. Katy would probably say I threw them into the water, which might be true, but I'm writing the story. The important thing is, they were gone. No amount of diving search and reconnaissance turned up a thread of her clothes.

"You idiot!" she fretted as Eve must have in the Garden of Eden when she realized she was naked. "Quit laughing!" My clothes dangled from my horse's bridle and she made a lunge for them. She wanted to toss my togs in the drink and watch them sink. Then we'd be even. "Let's see if you feel naked and unashamed when your clothes get sucked down by the monster under the water. I don't think you'll be laughing your stupid head off."

I was too quick for her and held my clothes tight as she made attempts to wrestle them away. "I'm not laughing *at* you! I'm laughing *with* you!"

"I'm not laughing," she retorted. But I saw a smile in the corner of her mouth all the same.

"Listen," I said, dodging a lunge she made for my shirt. "I'm your only hope. Without me you'll have to play Lady Godiva riding her horse with only your hair as a cover-up. And the only thing your hair covers is your ears! Think of me as your rescuer," I reasoned, as she seemed determined to have my clothes join the fate of hers. I envisioned Jemimah Puddle Duck and her sisters finding them somewhere down-river and going for a stroll with a blue bra over her wings. "Back off, or I'll leave you here," I said, swimming onto my mount and riding up the bank. "Hush! Somebody will come back here to see what all the caterwauling is if you don't quit squealing."

That shut her up. She looked around nervously as if the trees hid a million eyes. "I'll ride back and find something for you to wrap up in. No one will ever know," I promised lamely.

Katy sat on the horse with her knees pulled up under her chin. It was nearly impossible for her to keep her seat on her mare that way. She kept wobbling dangerously from one side to another.

"I'll be right back. I promise." I was tempted to ride back to Heathermoor and see what became of her, but she was my best friend and I wouldn't leave her naked.

I galloped to the trees near the fence that separated Mr Pool's pasture and the Cowarts' barn. Like a spy I waited and watched the barn door. All was quiet with no one in sight. I commando-crawled across the pasture, careful to dodge cow pies that lay scattered across my path. The cows eyed me with fascinated terror, no doubt wondering what this new creeping creature could be. I hoped they wouldn't stampede.

I scaled the fence with some difficulty. The top was laced with barbed wire. As I cleared the top something arrested my downward movement. Dang! I was stuck. I caught my belt loop on a barb, feet suspended inches from the ground. I twisted and turned like a scarecrow on a pole trying to unfasten myself. It reminded me painfully of an incident I thought I had forced from my memory – a horrible trauma I would most likely have to spend years in psychotherapy to forget again. I had only been in third grade, but the memory still brought a flush of shame to my already sun-burnt cheeks.

The boys had been chasing the girls on the playground. It was before I had learned to bite my fingernails and traumatize them. I and some other girls had been treed like possums. The girls with me jumped down and ran shrieking to another part of the playground. I jumped too but found myself in the same predicament I was in at present. Our school had a stupid dress code. It mandated the girls had to wear dresses. So instead of jumping down and making my getaway, my cute little dress caught on a branch. It pulled up over my head up to my eyeballs. Oh that it could have covered my eyes and I wouldn't have had to witness the horror.

There was a moment of silence on the playground. All the boys stopped running and stood with their heads cocked, mouths agape, staring at my panties. Several of them carried a hand full of monkey spears, a kind of prickly weed that sticks to your socks when walking through the woods. They lamely launched their weapons at my lacy underpants while I writhed and struggled, toes inches above terra firma.

I wriggled, bounced and twisted trying to free myself from this precarious position. After what seemed hours, but was probably only seconds of desperate struggle, my dress ripped and I crumpled to the ground, the laughter of the boys ringing in my ears.

The rest of recess I hid behind the school, totally humiliated! Katy sympathized with me and held my hand for support when I came out to face my public.

Remembering this episode, I redoubled my efforts to extricate myself from the fence and save her now.

After much bouncing and harrumphing, my belt loop popped, or the fence gave way, and I toppled ungracefully to the ground.

Miraculously no one appeared, but I thought I saw Mr Cowart in the hallway as I ran behind the barn.

Quietly I slunk into a stall on the outside of the barn. The horse Hmmhhmmed nervously. He turned and eyed me suspiciously. Wide white rims showed around his brown eyes as I scaled the side of his stall and disappeared in the hole in the ceiling above his hay rack.

Several barn cats, the progeny of the black mouser who had been at Heathermoor as long as anyone remembered, hung out in the hayloft looking for mice and acting like moody teenagers skipping class. I tiptoed around, trying my hardest to sound like a kitty and not a girl searching for a horse blanket. The only ones up there were the heavy winter ones. I was sure the scratchy wool would feel about as good as a sunburn on Katy's soft pink skin in the 90-degree weather. The summer blankets were down in the tack room. I couldn't chance bumping into Mr Cowart. He'd know something was up if I grabbed a blanket and hopped the fence to Mr Pool's. I had promised Katy I wouldn't tell.

The horse Mmmmhhhhmmmed a little louder when I came back through the hay rack. He was expecting a tuft of the sweet grass instead of my legs coming from the hole in the ceiling. Though my hair had the color and texture of the hay, he could tell it wasn't the real thing because it smelled like polluted creek water and was attached to my bony head. I crawled down, dragging the heavy blanket after me. I bundled it up in my best impression of a girl scout rolling her sleeping bag then scampered back to the fence with it tucked under my arm.

Behind me the booming voice of Mr Cowart shouted, "Mary! Mary! Mary Lou Buck what in the Sam Hill are you doing? Get back here right now!"

When an adult uses your full name you know you're in trouble. But my first allegiance was to Katy. I didn't even look back. In one leap I mounted my horse and galloped to my friend who was still perched on top of her mare.

"It took you long enough!" she complained. She grabbed the blanket and quickly concealed herself beneath it. "Yeoww, this is scratchy," she grumbled.

"Its better than fig leaves. Think about poor Eve," I laughed. "At least you're clothed and in your right mind, like the Gaderine demoniac after Jesus healed him. I bet they only had a blanket for him to wrap up in, too."

"That's so funny I forgot to laugh. Let's hurry back to the house before anyone sees me."

"I'm afraid it's too late for that," I said, doing my best to avoid eye contact. "I think I was discovered."

"Discovered! What'd you do, call the Birmingham News?" Katy's face, already red with the thought of someone knowing her shame, practically turned purple.

"Mr Cowart saw me when I escaped from Alcatraz."

"Mr Ccccc – M-m-m-mis-s-ster?"

There is nothing as modest as a pre-teen.

We tried to gallop past, but Katy's Southern upbringing of "Yes Ma'am's" and "Yes Sir's" was too strong a magnet when Mr Cowart yelled, "Stop, girls!"

He was standing at the fence waiting for us to pass by. Inevitably, it was the only way back. We'd lost the wire cutters. They had been in Katy's back pocket.

Up on the Roof

hen Franny dated my brother, Billy, she took me under her wing. She introduced me to "rock and roll." Perfect child that I was, I thought I'd die if I went against my parents' wishes. They frowned on rock music. They'd heard a popular Christian speaker say that rock and roll was a tool of the Devil's that boiled teenager's brains. He was probably right about most of it.

Franny took Simon and Garfunkle's song that said, "Your momma don't dance and your daddy don't rock and roll," to heart for me. She thought when I became a teenager I'd be left out because of my ignorance of rock and roll. She and my brother Billy gave me a proper education on tasteful rock music, from Emerson Lake and Palmer to the Beatles. She bought me *Sweet Baby James*, an early James Taylor record, and I wore the grooves off it.

I was thrilled to go anywhere with Franny. She was beautiful and stylish, no matter if she wore old jeans and a button-down men's shirt or the Papagallo sundresses that hugged her curves.

Once she took me to her family's compound to play the piano for a "tacky tea party" she threw for her high school friends. When the first guest arrived I was surprised to see an old woman with gray hair, thick eyeglasses and stockings bagging around her ankles. Though it was the middle of summer, a fox fur draped her neck. Its mouth had a little spring inside which bit its own tail to hold the stole in place.

"Wow," I asked, reaching to stroke it, "is that a real dog?"

When the woman laughed I realized she was just a teenager. Thick makeup and gray spray-in color had transformed her from a cute young thing into an old hag. Everyone else arrived in succession of tackiness, but no one topped the first girl.

I sat at the grand piano in the living room and played my recital pieces timidly. I felt silly and wanted to join the big girls who were having so much fun.

Afterward, Franny took me for a swim in her pool and told me the story of how she almost killed Love when they were only ten.

"First a little history lesson," she said. "You've heard people call Birmingham the 'Magic City?'"

I nodded.

"It earned this name by being the fastest growing city in the South. In the late 1960s people exited the downtown area and fled to the suburbs in droves. Mountain Brook people were old money – those who inherited it – and lived in mansions more like castles than houses. There were also folks who had gotten their money the old-fashioned way – by working for it. They wanted the status symbol of a Mountain Brook address, too. Building contractors made fortunes in house construction there.

"In the summer of 1967," Franny continued, "Love was ten and I was nine years old. We spent whole weeks at each other's houses, dragging our ponies along with us. Love was taller and didn't quite fit in my clothes, so we kept separate wardrobes at each other's place to avoid packing and unpacking."

I thought about Heathermoor, with its rambling house and grounds. It was magnificent by any standard, but the Cowart's financial situation wasn't what most people would expect of its inhabitants. Love must have felt the pressure of her precarious social position. She wrote in her diary, "I want to be rich and have a beautiful home with large green lawns and fine horses and an Irish Setter and a Persian cat and beautiful clothes and lots of flowers."

Going to Franny's gave Love a taste of the "rich" life.

"We were about your age when it happened," Franny continued as she floated in the cool blue water. "Love and I were the modern Lewis and Clark. Whether by ponies or on foot we loved to explore.

"It was summertime and I rarely wore shoes if I could help it. But practical Love wore hers as we tromped through the woods to explore a giant house that was going up next door."

Franny pointed toward the thickly wooded slope past the stable. "You can't see the place now, but in the winter you can see it through those trees over there."

The stable stood empty, looking forlorn since Boogaloo had taken up permanent residence at Heathermoor where Katy and I arm wrestled to see who would get to ride her.

Franny continued, "The soles of my feet were tough from going barefoot all summer and I didn't mind the sticks and rocks so much. But when we scrambled over the big ditch around the massive foundation of the new house, the area was littered with nails, broken bottles and shredded metal.

"Love took off one of her shoes and gave it to me. We threw our arms around each other and hopped from room to room like contestants in a three-legged race. It was so cool to walk through the big empty rooms and imagine how they would look when they were finished.

"A staircase went up and up to what would be the attic. We walked across the beams to look down the chimney. I still get the willies," she shivered, "remembering how we stared down the framed-in flue three stories to the basement. Sharp strips of tin jutted out the whole way down the dark tunnel. Like a vacuum it seemed to draw you forward into its depths.

"I stood on the roof and shouted, 'I'm queen of the world,' at the peasants below." Franny paused and looked in the direction of the house. Then she pointed, "Look through there, Mary. You can just see the roof above the trees."

I saw a faint outline of a massive roof-line.

"On the other side," Franny explained, "is a valley. Up on the roof we had a spectacular view. It was my idea. That's why I feel responsible for the accident. When you're a kid you think you're invincible. Love was my best friend; I loved her and never meant to hurt her. I wished it had been me."

I realized Franny was still punishing herself for something she was in no way responsible for. I tried to say this, but I was still just a little kid and didn't know how to frame my sentences. She smiled at my childish attempt to soothe then went on.

"Love and I shared our deepest secrets ever since we were five years old."

She smiled and her eyes seemed to lose focus and I thought she might have forgotten I was there. Then she began to sing softly, "On the roof it's peaceful as can be, and there the world below won't bother me. That's what I say! Keep on telling you that right smack dab in the middle of town, I found my paradise. It's trouble proof. That if this old world starts to getting you down, there's room enough for two up on the roof."

Her voice trembled. She was silent a couple of minutes, her eyes focused on something in the distance. With the back of her hand she dashed at them and forced a laugh.

"That song always chokes me up!" She paused a moment as if reluctant to continue.

"We were there for awhile. Maybe Love's legs fell asleep. I don't know why or how it happened. All I remember is that when we stood up to go — Love slipped."

She lay back in the water and stared at the sky. I was afraid she wouldn't tell me the rest of the story. I hoped if I were quiet she'd go on. The water swishing around me sounded loud in the silence. I felt awkward as if I was trespassing in her memories.

At last, Franny whispered, "It was awful. She didn't scream. She didn't make a sound. But her eyes..." Franny shivered in spite of the ninety degree heat. "Right before she went down that dark hole I saw the fear in her eyes.

"I screamed, 'Love! Oh my gosh! Love! Help! Help!'

"I ran, one foot bare and the other in her shoe, not caring if I stepped on a nail or glass. I screamed the whole way down the staircase.

"Back then nobody lived nearby to hear my cries. I didn't know what I was going to do. I couldn't leave Love to go for help, but I was afraid to go down in the basement. What if she was ... I didn't think anyone could survive falling three stories through that sharp metal onto broken concrete.

"When I got down to the main floor I saw what I thought must be an angel running toward me. When he got closer I ran to him, grabbed him by both arms and started babbling. I was screaming and crying, trying to explain. I must have sounded like I was speaking in tongues.

"The man got the gist of my gibberish and vaulted down the steps into the basement. I stood looking after him for a moment, frozen with fear. Then I jumped down too. Come what may I had to see my best friend. Was she alive?

"It was dark down there, but shafts of sunlight penetrated the roughed-in floors. In the corner was a black hole. A tiny crumpled heap lay in it like a pile of rags in the darkness. A sunbeam came in sideways and illuminated her face.

"The stranger bent over her broken body. He felt for a pulse with his first two fingers then began running his hands along the back of her neck as if he were checking for ticks. I wondered what he was doing. He lifted her gently as a baby and carried her up the steps to the ground floor. When he laid her down I saw her chest moving. She was unconscious, but breathing. I knelt down by her head and sobbed, 'Is she going to live, Mister.'

"He didn't answer, he just began calmly giving orders, 'Go get a pillow and blanket. If you can find an ace bandage, bring that, or some rope. I need something to stabilize her leg. Call your mother. And call an ambulance.'

"'Yes, sir!' I said and ran to do his bidding.

"It felt good to have something to do. I raced through the woods to my house screaming, 'Mom! Mom! Love fell off the house.'

"The Cowarts had had a string of bad luck at that time. Mrs Cowart was on crutches with a broken ankle. Mr Cowart had broken a collarbone when that crazy horse, Richelieu, reared up and fell over backwards on him. Even Peter had a broken finger. He'd slammed it in his rabbit cage.

"That day Mrs Cowart had hobbled out on her crutches to watch Mr Cowart and the boys rake the newly mown fescue with an old-fashioned hayrake that seldom worked. Mom tried and tried to call them. They rarely answered their phone and it was impossible to get a hold of them. Mom called the Willoughbys' farm down the road and Mrs Willoughby jumped in her car and drove the mile and a half to find them.

"Mrs Cowart got there before the ambulance. I ran to meet her and started bawling all over again. She had a hard time getting through the woods on those crutches. By that time Love was awake. She was crying in this high, heart-piercing wail. It killed me to hear it. I could tell by her face it killed Mrs Cowart too.

"My angel held out his hand to her saying, 'I'm Dr McDowell. Your daughter is an amazing child. She kept repeating, "God is my refuge and strength," as I was splinting her leg.' He explained that Love had broken both collarbones

68

and had a compound fracture of her left femur, just below the hip.

"I heard my mom explaining to Mrs Cowart later, 'Dr Holt McDowell is never home! He has a very busy practice. It's a miracle he was walking in the woods during the day. I'm sure his expertise saved her, or at least helped avoid many complications and certainly much agony.'

"I couldn't believe that Love wasn't cut in half by all those sharp pieces of tin that stuck out all down that flue," Franny shuddered and shook her head. "I thought she'd be mince meat. But the amazing thing was she didn't even have a scratch. Not a single one. She had the smoothest olive complexion. She looked like a movie star with those big doe eyes and her silky brown mane. If she had cut her face up, I'm sure her vanity couldn't have stood it."

Of course I wanted to know everything. I had a million questions, but Franny had told her part and I'd have to get the rest of it out of Mrs Cowart another time.

The Cowarts made a "girls room" upstairs in their home for the barn girls to spend long weekends and overnights. The staircase went up several steps, turned at a landing and continued to the rooms at the top. A hallway ran across the front of the house with doors that opened into a bathroom and two large bedrooms. The last room was ours.

Mrs Cowart, Katy and I worked to reclaim it from the storage area it had been. Two single beds were made up with fresh linens. A small table separated them with a lamp for reading late into the night. Mrs Cowart stocked the bookshelf with her treasured books she had enjoyed as a child.

It was there I first discovered Alec and *The Black Stallion*, *The Adventures of Mario*, and *Gentleman Jim*. On the flyleaves Mrs Cowart's faded signature, Nita Brown, was followed by another. Slightly crooked, childlike lettering progressed at a downward angle – Love.

I would touch her name as if it were holy. It made the story all the more special to know that she had read it.

I wasn't much for subtlety. When Katy and I spent the night I asked Mrs Cowart to tell me the rest of the story of Love's fall.

"Love had to lie in that hospital bed for eight long weeks. Her leg was suspended by a pin through her knee joint to a pulley above the bed and her head had to be below her body."

Mrs Cowart grimaced in describing her condition as if the memory brought back the horror.

"No way!" I couldn't believe it. "Eight weeks!"

"Mmhhmm," she nodded, "my baby, who loved the outdoors, riding all over creation day and night, had to be cooped up in a tiny sterile room for two whole months."

"What'd she do all that time? Watch TV?" I asked.

"TV bored her. She wanted to play table games with her dad or me. Mr Cowart couldn't stand to be away from his precious daughter. She was the light of his life. I'd stay with her until school was out, then he would come straight from work and stay till one of them fell asleep.

"She read a lot too. I was always amazed at her taste in literature. Even as a ten year old she loved the classics, unlike me as a little girl. I only read westerns. She also loved missionary biographies. Her aunt Barbara Barker kept her supplied with them from Briarwood Church's bookstore. Amy Carmichael's story was the first. Love devoured it quickly and Barbara realized she needed to bring more than one book at a time.

"A good deal of her reading was in the Bible. But a terrible thing happened because of it."

I couldn't imagine what terrible thing had been sparked from reading the Bible.

Mrs Cowart reached out and scratched Girl behind the ear. Girl was one of the original names the Cowarts had given their dogs. Girl wagged her behind along with her tail as if to say to the other dogs, "Look at me, I'm getting the love." Of course, all the other dogs – Pansy and Buddy and Job, the old dog who showed up one day covered in mangy sores – couldn't abide this kind of favoritism and pushed in for attention. Mrs Cowart lost her patience. "Git!" she scolded. The crowd of dogs obediently "got," and she continued her story.

"A young intern had accompanied the doctor on his examinations a few times. One afternoon he came in to check on Love by himself. Evidently, he had noticed her Bible-reading habit. 'Can't take it, huh?' he sneered. 'Always have to be reading that Bible, looking for a way out.'

"Then he turned his venom on me, 'You ought to be ashamed of yourself, teaching a child to escape like that,' he said, pointing at the Bible. Then he turned on his heel and stormed out.

"Both Love and I were shellshocked. I trembled all over and Love was in tears. At that time I hadn't matured in my walk with God enough to know that the young man wasn't lashing out against us, but against God. I experienced for the first time what people mean when they say, 'I was so mad I saw red.' I got so angry with that cruel intern that it seemed like everything in that hospital room was literally bathed in a crimson hue. How could he say such cruel things to a child who was obviously suffering? Looking back on it now, I feel sorry for him. I think he was scared. He didn't know God is the only true release from suffering and pain.

"Franny visited too. She kept us in stitches, outwitting the nuns with her illegal visits. The hospital had age limits for visitors and Franny was too young, but nothing could stop her from seeing her friend. And when Franny was around, nothing was ever dull.

"The man who rescued her, Dr McDowell, came by often. I think those two formed a special bond during their time alone after the accident. He was touched by her spirit and wrote her a beautiful letter about how she influenced him to see that God is truly our refuge and strength and ever-present help in trouble.

"After being in the hospital several weeks, Love began getting nervous. She picked at her covers restlessly. At first I couldn't figure out what was the matter. But when the nurse brought her lunch Love pleaded, 'No! I don't want that! Please, please, can't I just have a PJ?'

"The nurse stood in the doorway, tray in hand, eyes wide in a credible imitation of a deer in the headlights. 'Huh,' she responded eloquently.

"'I don't want that,' Love pointed at the offensive gray tray. 'I can't stand it anymore! All I want is a PJ.' She grew wilder as the nurse stood with the tray, staring open-mouthed.

"I came to the rescue of both, informing the nurse that a PJ was a peanut butter and jelly sandwich. Love disclosed that she was bothered by the three formal meals a day.

"This request threw the hospital staff into confusion. After a summit conference with the dietitian, the doctor, the hospital administrator and all manner of red tape they brought her a PJ and coke on the tray.

"'Not the tray!' Love practically screamed. 'Just wrap it in a napkin – no tray.'

"After two months in the hospital they let her come home. She wore a body cast from her armpits all the way down her right leg to her ankle. We loaded her in the back of the station wagon like a piece of furniture.

"Imprisoned in this straightjacket for six more months, we tried to make the best of it for her. Mr Cowart made a chaise-longue with wheels and the boys would roll her around the farm. The chair was too unwieldy for Franny so she pulled her around in a little red wagon. She'd march up and down the long white drive pulling Love out to get the mail. Sometimes when she'd run too fast the wagon would get a high speed wobble and Love would yell, 'Stop! Stop! I'm falling out.' Franny would shove her back in place, pull her up to the door and announce, 'Love's laughing so much she's gonna wet her cast. Bring out the bed pan!'"

Heart's Desire

*T*wo things made spring at Heathermoor special. The first was the flowers. As the farm originally had been a cultivated garden, the pasture became a palette of blue, white and yellow. The flowers brushed the ponies knees saying, "Sh, sh, sh," as we carved paths through them.

The other was that the mares foaled. Baby horses appeared overnight, as if the stork delivered them to the happy mares who smiled proudly at their offspring.

It takes over eleven months for a mare to produce a foal and the last few uncertain weeks seem like an eternity. Katy and I never got to see one being born since they prefer having their foals at night in strict secrecy. It's rare that a mare needs help, but when she does, it's usually a matter of life and death.

Mr and Mrs Cowart knew if they were going to really be in the horse business they would need a good stud horse — one with a recognizable name that would draw people to buy his offspring. Mrs Cowart dreamed of buying Blanchita's Society Rex, owned by their friend, Bob Smith.

They met Bob a few years before when they trailered one of their new mares to his farm to breed with Rex. Bob had taken the Cowarts under his wing. "Breed the best with the best and hope for the best," he was fond of saying.

Earlier that same year Bob turned down an offer of $30,000 for his stud horse. That was more than the selling price of the Cowarts' first Mountain Brook home – an enormous sum for the 1960s – so there seemed little hope that Rex would ever be theirs.

They began looking at a two year old colt whose pedigree was as impressive as any horse alive. Every sire and dam in his family had been a champion for the last fifty years. They decided to go see him. If he were anything close to their expectations they would buy him.

When Mr Cowart called his owner to make an appointment the man had a sudden reversal. "I've decided not to sell. He's just too well bred and it would be foolish of me to part with him."

The Cowarts didn't know what to do. It seemed like all the doors had slammed in their face. Maybe they weren't meant to breed horses after all. The time to breed the mares was almost here.

A month later they received an unexpected phone call. Apparently the owner of the well-bred colt had a change of fortune. "All my help has left me," he said abruptly. "I can't keep up the barn. If you still want to buy Marine Denmark, I'll knock $500 off his price!"

Mr Cowart picked up Love and shoved her in the back of the station wagon and sprinkled the boys around her. The whole family made the long trip to Memphis to get the stallion. Seeing a high-stepping two year old out in the pasture, the Cowarts immediately recognized Denmark from his description.

Mike and Richard hoisted Love up so she could see the dark liver chestnut. He was almost black, with a carrot-colored mane. Denmark was still young and gawky but had a good trot and the gentle disposition of his sire, Marine Ace. Mr Cowart carried Love over to stroke him. He snorted at the strange-looking stiff child, but submitted to her caresses. Eventually he forgot his fear and curiosity took over as he snuffled her ear. Love giggled. She was captivated.

Denmark was still a young, unproved stallion. There were doubts that as a coming three year old he could even get mares in foal. Thankfully, he didn't seem to have any trouble in that department, but they would have to wait a long time to see how his foals would turn out.

One Saturday night during this waiting period the Cowarts got a call from Bob Smith. He was in a rage. Bob considered horses to be equal with people, thereby deserving his moral judgments. Rex, the $30,000 stallion, had gone crazy, injured a mare and run through a fence after Bob. Bob took it personally.

"John," he said over the phone, "if you get up here today, I'll give you Rex."

"You're joking!" Mr Cowart replied incredulously.

"If you don't take him, I'll blow his brains out!"

Mr Cowart knew Bob wouldn't shoot the horse but thought he'd better get up there quick before he changed his mind about giving him away. Hours later he returned to Heathermoor with their heart's desire, an incredible gift.

That evening, after dressing the wounds the stallion had gotten from his stunt at Bob's, the Cowarts closed the door on another miracle – the horse that cost more than a house.

The next morning they let him out for exercise. Rex trotted up and down the fence line with his head high and nostrils quivering. He stopped abruptly and fixed his eyes on something only he could see in the distance. His copper coat glistened in the sun and his long neck stretched up like a swan. With ears so sharp they practically touched, he looked every inch the champion that he was. Mrs Cowart's arms broke out in goose bumps.

Months earlier a famous horse photographer had driven all the way from California to take his picture. It was obvious why Rex was rated fifth out of hundreds of horses in *Saddle and Bridle* magazine's famous sire rating of American Saddlebreds. They award points according to size and prestige of shows in which the stallions had competed and honors they had won.

He began to trot, whinnying loudly, knees high and tail flagging up over his back. He was calling the mares who would be his harem. He paced up and down the fencerow for a moment then reared as if he were about to jump.

At that moment the Cowarts' world crumbled. In disbelief they watched their miracle fall to pieces. Rex's back legs collapsed.

Mrs Cowart froze, unable to breathe as she watched the great horse writhe on the ground. Mr Cowart rushed forward as Rex thrashed and strained to get up. Then the proud horse lay still, breathing hard, as if he knew he was finished.

"His pelvis is broken in three places," the vet said, giving the diagnosis. "There is no possible way the horse will ever stand again. Every time he thrashes, those bone ends damage more muscle. Any moment his spinal cord will be severed. There's no hope for this horse. He must be destroyed."

Even the Auburn Vet School had no advice to offer, except to echo, "Destroy the horse."

They gave Rex several tranquilizers and sat up with him all night. Mrs Cowart couldn't believe their gift had been snatched away.

"Why, God, did you give us this horse only to take him back?" she shouted, shaking her fist at heaven. "How could you tease us like this if you weren't really going to let us have him?"

Stars winked in the darkness, but God didn't speak.

She rested her head on Mr Cowart's broad shoulder and cried softly. Through her tears a thought came into her head, "What do you love more, the gift or the giver?"

She received the chastisement. Like Job of old she prayed, "I trust you Lord, though you slay me, I trust you."

Necessity being the mother of invention, Mr Cowart rigged a canvas sling and, with the help of a neighbor with a wrecker, moved Rex to the barn. With great care they got him into a stall where he hung in the ingeniously designed device that supported the bulk of his weight while allowing his feet to barely touch the ground for balance. Rex seemed to recognize that the Cowarts were trying to help him. He cooperated fully.

Though the experts continued the same gloomy advice, "Put him to sleep!" the Cowarts persevered. Rex retained his fire, holding his head high, eyes blazing.

Love, newly emerged from her body cast, had special empathy for Rex. Her leg had healed but the femur just below the hip was permanently bowed. She would limp into Rex's stall to curry and brush him. He loved being groomed since he couldn't roll or do anything for himself. Love spent a lot of time obliging him. She well-remembered the boredom of being trapped in a small room.

As she brushed him daily they formed a bond. It grieved her to watch his chestnut hide stretch tighter and tighter over his protruding bones. He lost a lot of muscle in the months of hanging in the stall. But he became adept in manipulating his sling and moved with ease wherever he wanted.

"He looks just like the monkeys in the zoo swinging on their swings," Love said, laughing.

Gradually Rex's hind legs took more of his body weight. Finally the day came when they dropped the pressure of the sling entirely. He moved gingerly in his stall at first, then after weeks of waiting he was ready to come out.

Like Love, who was confined for such a long time, Rex had to learn to walk again. Mr and Mrs Cowart steadied the near-skeleton horse on either side, balancing him with their hands as he weaved and swayed. It reminded Mrs Cowart of Love's first unsteady steps.

Love, too, was very aware of the similarities between herself and the stallion. She sat on the fence and watched her parents help him as they had helped her. Like the king he was named for, Rex held his great head high and regal. He never deigned to look left or right, as if he were unaware of his pitiful condition and the Cowarts' support.

During Rex's convalescence, the vet, Barbara Benhart, was impressed by the success of the sling. She and Mr Cowart made two more slings and together saved several other horses by the same method.

Denmark's colts, lively as sprites, came that spring. The miracle of birth was everywhere as the foals greeted the world in amazement. All the wonder of the world would imprint itself on the clean slate of their newly awakened selves. Eyes that had never seen, lungs that never breathed, legs that never walked and ears that never heard would suddenly be thrust into the fullness of life.

The ability to immediately stand, see and hear sets horses apart from human babies or even puppies that grow gradually into awareness of the external world. Mrs Cowart could hardly get anything done for watching them play. She and Love would sit in the pasture and wait for them to come investigate. They'd stretch out tiny soft muzzles and snort sweet baby breaths on their faces. The colts' long curling whiskers tickled Love and made her laugh.

Mrs Cowart would cautiously reach out to scratch their rumps. She'd dig her fingers into their fuzzy hides and rub hard near their tails. After two or three good scratches they'd be enslaved. It delighted Love to watch the colts' noses trace circles in the air with their upper lips twitching in delight.

Slowly Rex regained strength. Love cheered when he was able to trot. She felt bound to him in some way. Watching his recovery was like having an out-of-body experience, as if she was able to view herself going through her own confinement and recovery all over again.

The part of his pelvis that was supposed to sever the spinal cord had fused around it, causing his back to be permanently rigid. Rex moved stiffly, but he could move. He could trot. And he could do the one job assigned him on this earth – he could breed.

Gradually, the flesh began to creep back between his bones and hide. After more than eight months, the same amount of time Love spent in the hospital and in the body cast, Rex was back. That year they bred all the mares to him. Every single mare came in foal, their stomachs growing larger as the months marched by.

But Rex remained a mystery. He loved human company but pinned his ears back and threw himself violently against the wall every time a horse passed his stall. The Cowarts began to understand why he had become such a burden to his former owner.

"He's not a burden," Love defended him. "Easy, boy," she'd say, and stroke his neck.

Rex and Love seemed connected in a way that no one else could understand. Love would scold him, "You've got to quit this Rex, you idiot. You're going to kill yourself!"

After a year of his crashing into the wall Mrs Cowart noticed that Rex had difficulty extending his left forefoot. The injury appeared to be in the radial nerve in his shoulder. His condition worsened, compounded by other symptoms of his back injury.

One day Mrs Cowart found Rex standing in his stall. He didn't greet her with his usual neigh and fiery look. His head was down. "John, come here," she called, her voice quavered and tears welled in her eyes.

When Mr Cowart saw the proud horse hanging his head he looked at his wife. They both knew it was time to release Rex from the prison his body had become.

Mrs Cowart was afraid how Love would react to the death of the horse she had so identified with, but she never spoke a word about it. The private child kept her secrets in her heart, not revealing them to anyone but God.

"Most people never knew that one of the finest sires of the American Saddle Horse breed was gifted to a couple of nobodies who believed in prayer," Mrs Cowart said, "and that he died in Leeds, Alabama."

After eleven long months of waiting, spring came, bringing Rex's first and only crop of colts. Each one was a gift, the last of his line. They were pretty little things with the long neck and the bright eyes of their sire.

One mare, Sparkle, who Mike trained and Love won blue ribbons on, was waiting on her first-born from Rex. Love kept watch every day with much anticipation for the foal. Every day Mrs Cowart checked to see if Sparkle's udder was swollen. It finally began to bulge, signifying the time was near, perhaps a week away.

After several more days Love got up one morning and went to check on the mare. In the distance she heard a horse neighing frantically. Her heart froze. She ran through the secret garden and climbed the fence into the front pasture. Sparkle ran around the group of mares, whinnying, then cantered down to the bank of the lake. She called again in a loud neigh then ran back up to the mares. Love watched her do this several times before realization dawned. Sparkle had foaled but couldn't find her baby.

"Oh, God, no," Love whispered. Then she bolted back to the house screaming the whole way, "Mom! Dad!"

Her parents came running when they heard her shouts. "Something's wrong!" she panted, "With Sparkle. She's going crazy and looking for her baby."

Pulling on boots Mrs Cowart went out in her bathrobe. The boys in pajamas and their dad half-dressed all joined in to search the pasture. Looking behind each of the limestone rocks jutting out of the ground, Love hoped against hope they'd find the little creature. There was a chance they could save it if they found it soon enough.

Rain began falling in large, heavy drops. Everything became wet and gray. Love hardly noticed. It was eerie hearing the mare screaming for her baby, her hoofbeats never stopping their pounding around the pasture. Sparkle ran to Mrs Cowart. She bumped her muzzle against her shoulder as if to ask, "Have you seen my baby?"

Finally Love called, "Mom, Dad! Over here." She was standing about ten feet from the bank of the lake. Love pushed the wet hair out of her eyes.

"Look," she said and pointed. Rain streamed down her somber face and dripped off her nose and chin.

From marks on the bank it was obvious that the foal in its thrashing to get on its feet had fallen down the steep bank into the lake where it was swallowed by the water. They searched the surface for any sign of a body, but the lake had apparently pulled it under.

Sparkle kept her vigil, calling for her little one who would never answer.

Two weeks later the Cowart boys fished the tiny skeleton of the foal out of the spillway.

Parachute Landing
Fall

*T*he summer of 1976 we celebrated the bicentennial at school with a musical. Our class sang several old songs from the turn of the century. I got to be the girl who was taken out to the ball game and bought peanuts and crackerjacks. I didn't care if we ever came back for it's "root, root, root for the home team..." We wore long dresses and wondered how girls went to baseball games in long dresses. When I went to my brother's football game Katy and I wore blue jeans and spent the whole game sliding down a muddy hill behind the bleachers. The government celebrated by coining a commemorative quarter and other such hoopla in Washington. I didn't pay much attention because most of my brain, as you may remember, was taken up with thoughts of horses. But it did strike me as unfair that my parents made me go to school, since one family we knew pulled their kids out. They stayed home because they thought Jesus was going to come back and take them up in the rapture that year. Why bother going to school if you are going to heaven instead? I do recall seeing them later on in January or February. Bummer for them.

I was thirteen years old, practically grown up. My class read George Orwell's book, *1984*. Big Brother was a scary concept for a seventh grader and I wondered what the future would hold. At the barn a boisterous girl with a wide smile, and a mouth to boot, joined our posse. Nancy King rode a little paint pony with an original name – Spot. We were fond of saying, "See Spot run. Run Spot run!" as Nancy chased him around the field with a halter and bucket of feed.

After catching all the ponies and horses the games would begin.

"Uh uh, I'm not the cowboy," Nancy said, chewing on a lock of hair.

"You'll get worms that way," Katy said. She pointed her double-jointed index finger at Nancy. "I used to chew my hair and got tapeworms – nasty things."

"Nancy, you have to be the cowboy because you're the only one with a western saddle." I thought the conversation digressed and didn't want to hear ... again ... how Katy had discovered her tapeworms.

"You use it!" Nancy was spitting violently to expectorate the worms.

Somehow God gave boys all the spitting genes. When girls spit, it just drools off our lower lips in a long wet line.

Nancy wiped her mouth and said, "I've got a real Indian pony and none of you do. I have to be an Indian."

"Well, I have to be the Indian princess, because I can swing up better than everyone else," I stated proudly. "Katy, you have to be the cowboy."

"Aw, I don't want to ride in a saddle. Can't we all be Indians?" she begged. "I hate getting scalped and the cowboy always gets scalped. It hurts! Last time you took your role a little too seriously. I've got a hole in the top of my head where you pulled a chunk of my hair out," she fingered the spot and grimaced.

"If I'm the princess, I won't scalp you. Nancy will." This was as close as I got to an apology.

Nancy eyed Katy's brown hair with a little wicked gleam. Katy put her hand over it protectively.

"Okay, Katy, you can go bareback. It'll save time anyway. You're still the cowboy though. Start chasing Nancy across the pasture up by Mr Pool's fence. Be sure and count to ten before you go. Count slow ... one Mississippi, two Mississippi, three Mississippi ... don't rush it.

"I'll be down by the creek. And Nancy, don't take so long to rescue me. I got eaten up by mosquitoes last time." I always made up the rules. Although Nancy and Katy were good improv players, my imagination ran wilder.

Today we were playing on the ponies. I trudged down to the creek, watching for snakes. I never saw one, but my dad hammered it in my head to watch where I stepped. Alabama's got some nasty pit vipers.

"Help! Help!" I shouted in my best Indian maiden in distress voice, when I saw Nancy coming close. She slowed to a fast trot and I jogged beside Spot trying to swing up. "Slow down a little more," I said.

"Hurry! Here comes the cavalry," Nancy urged.

I swung up behind her and away we flew. I clung to Nancy, looking back to see Katy following close behind.

"If I touch you, you're the cowboy!" Katy shouted as she cantered nearer.

"Go up the enduro!" I commanded Nancy. The enduro was a motorcycle trail the Cowart boys had cut through the dense undergrowth to the right of the middle pasture. When I was a little girl I watched my brother, Billy, ride a long enduro motorcycle race there. The trail crossed a creek that fed the lake in the front pasture. Heading uphill it made a winding circuit through the trees until it spat back out on the other side of the woods into the pasture again.

If we could gain a little distance Nancy and I could ambush Katy. But riding double and jumping a creek at the same time was a recipe for disaster. Spot, not the most fluid jumper at best, slammed on the brakes, throwing me into Nancy's back. Then he gathered his nerve and crow-hopped across the ditch. I grabbed Nancy for purchase, but she was unsettled by the quick stop and go Spot had executed. We both toppled off backwards and landed in a tangle of arms and legs in the creek.

Spot kept going. He galloped up the hill as if he didn't even notice he'd lost his riders. Katy jumped off her pony and whooped, "Aaaiiiyaayaayaa!" Reaching down, she unmercifully jerked both Nancy's and my hair at the same time.

"You're scalped!" she crowed. "Hey ya ya ya, hey ya ya ya," she chanted and executed a victory dance, stomping the shallow water vigorously splashing our faces.

"Get off me!" Nancy shoved. "You pulled me off!"

Taking no notice of Nancy's accusation I shouted, "You're the cowboy Katy! They don't take scalps. They shoot you." I was trying to preserve the sanctity of the game.

"Bam, bam!" Katy yelled, shooting imaginary pistols. Her pony threw his head and backed up suddenly. The reins were looped around her arm and she was jerked off her feet.

Nancy and I were bruised, but this was too great an opportunity to pass up. We both scrambled up the bank after her, but Katy was too quick. By the time we got there, she was mounted and trotting away with her thumb in her ear and the other four fingers wagging at us.

Spot emerged at the other end of the woods and trotted back to join his pasture buddies. He began pulling up grass and munching contentedly, not at all minding the bit in his mouth.

"Come here, Katy. Give us a ride." Katy rode up to the fence and Nancy and I clambered on. All three of us rode back while Katy sang, "Git along little doggies." She had won the day.

"Rats!" Nancy hissed.

"What's wrong?" I asked.

Nancy held up a tattered rein. "He must have stepped on it."

My first horse, Big Man, had recently undergone something of a nervous breakdown. He refused to run or jump possibly because of arthritis or maybe he was just plain tired. I got a new horse named Lovely. I was thrilled to have a horse that could gallop in a flat-out run and beat the other girls' short-legged ponies in races. She was green, meaning she was young and not super broken-in. But I was invincible and believed I could ride anything. I didn't figure out that wasn't true until it was too late.

Lovely hated it when you touched her ears. When I tried to slip the bridle over them she would thrust her head up so high I had to climb the fence to do it.

"Shoot!" I said to Nancy who held up Spot's tattered rein. "That's nothin', Lovely broke three this week. Did you notice the split rail propped up on the gate by the house?" I jerked my head in the direction. "Lovely busted that and a rein yesterday. I hadn't tied her up for a second before she started backing up like that fence was electrified."

"You better watch it," Nancy warned. "Your horse isn't half broke!"

"You're just jealous 'cause she's faster than Spot. I understand Lovely. She loves me!" I threw my arms around her neck. She snorted and half-reared.

"See! See! You better watch out." Nancy huffed as she jumped on Spot belly first then swung her right leg over his back grunting with an effort.

"Watch and learn," I bragged, grabbing Lovely's chestnut mane and swung up in one fluid motion.

Katy emerged from the barn with our sack lunches. We planned to go up to the house and eat on the back porch. It was at least ten degrees cooler in the shade of the elms.

"Here ya go," she said handing me my lunch. She swung up on her pony and we three headed up the gravel road to the house.

"What'd ya'll bring," I asked.

"I got a peanut butter and pickles sandwich," Katy said.

"Ewww! Disgusting," Nancy and I chorused.

"The pickles keep the peanut butter from sticking to the roof of your mouth. It's not bad. Don't knock it till you try it." She rolled her eyes at Nancy who was leaning over Spot's neck pretending to throw up.

"And monster cookies," Katy added. Nancy sat up and grinned ingratiatingly at her. Monster cookies were chocolate chip cookies with other good things thrown in for fun: those colorful candies that melt in your mouth and not in your hands, raisins, oatmeal. They were big enough for a monster too.

"I'll be your best friend if you give me one," I promised.

"I've heard that before," Katy opened her bag, pulled out the cookies and spit on each of them. "You can have one now if you want it."

"You're so selfish. Just for that you can't have any of my delicious lunch." My mom packed the most boring lunches, usually PJs with whatever fruit was in season. Rarely did I get cookies or treats.

Mom had the popular condition of the day – hypoglycemia. It seemed every other lady at church had it too. Since her diagnosis, she had made me go to the doctor to see if I had it too. I had to drink this nasty, thick, sugary substance in a green bottle. I gagged after every swallow. It was enough to make anybody's blood sugar revolt. Thirty minutes later they stuck me full of needles, drawing blood by the gallon. As a result mom packed me "healthy lunches."

Maybe today would be different. I hoped. Crackling open the paper bag to see what was inside was the last thing I remember cohesively. Ground, sky and horse whirled in a mad palette of green, brown and blue.

The next thing I knew Mr Cowart was leaning over me. "Mary! Mary! Are you all right?" I have a vague recollection of seeing fireworks explode in brilliant flashes around his head when I first opened my eyes. "This is why they make cartoon characters see fireworks," I whispered. Episodes like this must have been what turned Mr Cowart's hair prematurely gray. Lovely was long gone.

"How many heads do I have," Katy called over his shoulder.

"Hush," Mr Cowart chided. He picked me up.

Mr Cowart was as strong as the horses he worked, and I wasn't embarrassed to be carried like a baby back to the barn. He smelled good – like horse sweat, hay and aftershave.

"What happened?" I wondered aloud.

"Lovely did a cartwheel," Nancy volunteered.

"More like a back flip," Katy countered.

"I was afraid something like that would happen," Mr Cowart said. My head bobbed against his chest as he walked. "Lovely's still green. You shouldn't ride her and crackle paper bags at the same time." I thought I felt his chest wiggle. Was he laughing at me?

I found out little by little a lot of things scared Lovely, but I was more prepared and didn't get thrown again, at least by her. She was an exciting horse and a darn good jumper. We girls would have impromptu jumping contests. Grabbing the mane we'd leap bareback over fences, logs, creeks, anything worthy of jumping. Whoever cleared the highest thing got bragging rights.

One day while riding to a neighbor's farm we came upon a tree lightning had struck. The bark was stripped clean off, denuding it. Long strands of the tender cambium lay like shrapnel on the ground. The giant had snapped about four feet off the ground, its trunk stretching out long in open invitation.

Katy jumped off to get a rough idea of its height, and then the betting began.

"I bet Roxy can clear it," she challenged. Not having a horse of her own, she always rode a different mount. Today it was a little red chestnut named Roxy.

Mounting, Katy trotted Roxy back for a running start and cantered swiftly at her target. Roxy bolted sideways at the last minute, almost sending Katy over the tree sans horse. But she held on barely. Shaken but not stirred, she tried again. This time Roxy nearly sat down as she skidded to a stop in front of the trunk.

"Lovely won't refuse," I said, hoping I was right. We turned our backs to the tree to taxi down the runway and prepare for take off. I patted her neck and gave her a pep talk. "You can do it girl. I know you can." As we turned for the approach I leaned over and whispered, "Extra sweet feed when we get home if you make it."

We were bareback as usual. When you relaxed and thrust your legs forward you could trot for hours. We started trotting. I wasn't going to go too fast at first. I clucked with my tongue in the side of my mouth and Lovely broke into an easy canter.

Thud up, thup, thup, thud up, thup, thup. Her hooves beat in time with my heart. As we got closer I leaned forward, grabbed her mane and encouraged, "Come on girl, you can do it. Come on Lovely!"

Whoosh! We were airborne. There's nothing like the feeling of weightlessness. I was flying. I looked down at all the lowly people below, knowing I was queen.

Katy, Nancy and I practiced all kind of useless stunts. One was perfecting the art of falling. We'd canter up the hill in the back pasture and practice. My brother, Billy, and Richard Cowart had taken up skydiving. Billy explained to me in detail how you land a parachute. "It's called P.L.F. That stands for Parachute Landing Fall. You hit the ground with your feet and roll side-ways like this." He demonstrated by jumping off the couch. He landed on his feet then collapsed sideways in a roll.

Katy and I figured if the technique worked with parachutes it should work with horses too. We developed the H.L.F., Horse Landing Fall. Leaping off our speeding mounts, we'd try to land on our feet and roll sideways.

The hardest part was making the first jump. "You first," I said to Katy as we galloped uphill.

"No, you."

We reached the top, neither of us being brave enough to jump. Finally, we decided to do it together. Misery loves company. I guess stupidity does too.

"Ready! Set! Go!"

We started up the hill again.

"Slow down a little," I suggested. We pulled back to a slow canter. "Okay on three. One – two – awe!"

We had reached the top again.

"This time, this time," we promised each other.

We rode to the base of the hill again.

"Go!" The horses had the hang of it and were pulling at the bits to run up the hill again. "This is it!" I shouted, "One! Two! Threeee!" We both jumped at the same time rolling in a wild tangle of arms and legs. I lay for a moment looking at the sky, making an inventory of my bones.

Katy sat up. "Are you okay?" she asked.

I sat up too. We grinned. "That was so cool! Let's do it again."

The only problem was that the horses had run away. We spent an hour chasing them down.

"Next time let's jump one at a time. First you ride beside me holding Lovely with a lunge line," I said as the horses ran past us for the fifth time. "That way you can keep her from running away. Then I'll hold Big for you."

After perfecting this feat we'd ride down the side of the county highway together. Cantering in perfect unison, one of us would fall from our mount while the other kept going. I was the first to do it and looked forward to practicing my acting skills.

A car sped up behind us and I jumped executing a perfect H.L.F. I lay on the ground not moving. I think I even hung my tongue out the side of my mouth, doing my best imitation of a dead dog. Our third "man," Nancy, waited at the end of the pasture on the other side of the fence to see if the car would stop. The first couple of tries the cars sped on. Those Pharisees! Where was our Good Samaritan?

Finally one slowed to a stop and backed up. When it reached me I heard the hhhmmmm of the electric window. "Hey, are you okay?" someone called.

"Dang, I think she's dead!" I heard him say to his companion.

About the time their car door clicked and creaked to open, I heard the thumpety, thumpety, thump of Spot's hooves running to the rescue. I jumped up, surprising my would-be rescuers, climbed the fence and vaulted onto Spot's back. Nancy barely slowed enough for me to make it.

"Sucker!" she yelled back as we dashed through the field, jumping a downed fence at the other side.

Katy joined us, leading Lovely. "That was hilarious! What'd they say?" she asked.

I recounted the whole story and we all had a good laugh on the Good Samaritan.

One day Lovely began to refuse fences, even tripping over small logs. She stopped galloping and turned into an ornery old puss. I lost interest in her because she became a party-pooper.

It was springtime and the "babies" were blooming, so we started playing with the foals. They were so cute and leggy. Their muzzles were velvet and their manes downy feathers.

There were all ages of colts and fillies on the farm, from newborn to yearling and up. When we girls started showing an interest Mr and Mrs Cowart saw free labor. I'm not too sure how much we helped at first, but we became apprentice horse-breakers and there were lots of horses to practice on.

Franny told me when she and Love helped break colts the Cowart boys would help wearing their football helmets. Catching unbroken colts to put halters on them could be a harrowing experience. They'd go into a stall with a frightened colt, which might run over anyone in its way. Considerable struggling, banging and crashing resulted. Finally, someone would get an arm around the colt's neck and another under its tail hoisting it up over its back. This was the only way you could hold it while someone else put the halter on.

After observing this rough maneuver, one friend told Mrs Cowart, "Now I see why your boys are such good football players."

Mrs Cowart just smiled. She knew they were such good colt wrestlers because nearly every night since they were born they had rolled and wrestled with their daddy, usually in the middle of the living room floor. The price she paid was frayed nerves — she couldn't stand physical violence — and the loss of many wedding presents. Years later when Katy and I would spend the night with them, we'd see the hidden bricks supporting furniture that had crumbled beneath the onslaught of past wrestle-manias.

Katy and I tried colt wrestling, though we didn't wear football helmets as the Cowart boys had done years before. Mr Cowart helped us, always taking the brunt of the colts when they dove and bucked. We'd be ready to slip the halters over their head. We spent hours leading the babies around and lunging the bigger ones.

I started taking riding lessons with Jeannie Cox, who said I had the best seat of anyone she had ever seen. I'm not sure how many seats she had seen, but I took it as high praise. When I wasn't at the barn I would stand around at home, squeezing a basketball between my knees because Jeannie said it would strengthen my grip muscles.

One day after I led one of the colts around the barn, Mr Cowart called, "Mary! Come here a minute."

He was standing in the corner of a stall with one of the two year olds. I had seen him lunging this one earlier with a dumb-jockey. A dumb-jockey has a wooden contraption in the shape of an x that is buckled onto the horse like a saddle. It gives the horse the feel of something upright on his back as he trots around on the lunge line.

"Hop up. I want to see what he does." Mr Cowart grabbed my knee and boosted me onto the colt. I guess I was the dumb jockey now.

"Just lay on him, don't try to sit up."

I was so excited to be the first person to ever get on that horse. I was making history. Mr Cowart led the horse slowly around the stall, whispering encouragements.

"Okay Mary, ease your leg over. Stay low."

I could feel the horse's muscles tense under me and wondered if I'd hit the roof of the stall if he bucked. He trembled all over as if some beast of prey perched on his back to devour him. I rubbed his neck and spoke soothingly, "Good boy, its okay. That's it."

Mr Cowart led me in small circuits around the stall.

This began my initiation of bronc busting. I don't know why it's called that. The only thing that busted was me when I flew off. Usually with much handling and gentle persuasion the horses were nervous, but not wild. I loved it. You couldn't have kept me away from them if you tried.

The next step in horse-breaking would take place in the small round ring. Mr Cowart put the horse on a long lunge line, held him tight and then helped me up. We'd follow the same pattern: lie astride, ease my leg over, keep low. Eventually I'd sit up and trot around the circle.

Mr Cowart stood in the center holding the lunge line and a long whip. He'd call instructions, "Okay, now pull him up and walk. Easy, easy. That's good." The nervous colt responded to me. I was amazed. His ears would flick back and forth as if he could see me with them, and I felt his body rigid and tense under the saddle. "All right, ask him to trot. No! Don't kick him!" I suddenly found myself racing around the ring on a galloping, bucking colt.

I was thrown more than a few times. But I even loved that. Everything was exciting. I wanted Mr Cowart to think I was tough so he'd let me ride more horses than Katy or Nancy. He'd say, "If you fall off three times you're an expert." If that was true I was a super expert. But I was sticking on more and more and it got harder and harder for them to throw me.

In the late 1970s, mechanical bulls were popular. In Texas clubs had machines that acted like bucking broncos. This phenomenon was popularized by the John Travolta movie, *Urban Cowboy*, which I never saw. But the commercials for it sparked my imagination. Mostly drunk guys full of testosterone would climb on and say something like, "Hey bubba, watch this!" before they flew off and broke both arms.

Even so I was dying to try it. A bar in downtown Birmingham had one of these machines, but I couldn't convince my parents to let me go down there and take a ride. By the time I got my driver's license, even though I peeled up the side and changed my birthday to make me old enough to get in, it was too late. The mechanical bull was passé.

The Cowarts convinced my parents I was ready for a show horse. We sold Lovely, who had become sickly. She just stood around the pasture looking gloomy. We purchased Jericho, a big seal-brown gelding, to show as a pleasure horse. About three weeks after I got Jericho the reason why Lovely had soured was discovered. Everything made sense then – why she refused fences, why she stopped running, why she had become lethargic. She had been in foal!

Eleven months earlier she'd snuck in the back pasture with the other brood mares and had had a secret rendezvous with Denmark, the stud horse. Like some teenage girl, she had kept her secret right up to the end. If I'd only kept her three more weeks I'd have had my own baby to break!

Duct Tape on Doors

*S*how horses and see the world – or at least every little Podunk town in the southeast. I liked training and working the horses, but for me, horse shows were the pinnacle. A few were big events that lasted several days. At these we'd move the horses into a makeshift stable hastily constructed at the arena. Each barn decorated the sides of their stalls with their colors and banners to designate their area and make the riders proud. Daily we'd pin up the ribbons we accrued from each class to show how well Heathermoor's horses were doing. I loved donning my riding kit and strutting up and down slapping my crop against the side of my leg in an authoritative manner.

But most of the shows we went to were one-day affairs. People from big and small barns caravanned from all over the state, pulling horse trailers to tiny places like Hueytown, Georgiana, Columbiana and several other "...ana's" whose names have become a blur in my memory. These shows were usually held on the local high school football field. Horse trailers parked helter-skelter in the gravel lot nearby; it made me think of the place as a giant gypsy camp. At these small shows, there would be classes for Saddlebreds, Walking horses, Quarter horses and Arabians. We were snobs, thinking every horse outside the Saddlebred breed was inferior. How we wished only Saddlebreds populated the shows. We never deigned to watch any other class beside the ones with the "good" horses.

We'd show in several classes from early morning to late at night. The classes were accompanied by tinny organ music played by the local church organist or piano teacher who sat on a platform in the center of the ring.

The music changed as the announcer called out each command to the riders. "Walk," the announcer would call. The organist played something that sounded like, "Happy trails to you, until we meet again," the song echoing the horse's step. The music became livelier with the call to "trot," and the organist practically rocked out when they called "canter." This accompaniment reminded me of how music fit the mood in silent movies, the piano playing slow trills at sad parts and the William Tell Overture during chase scenes.

Getting to horse shows was half the fun, except for the first few shows I attended when my parents drove me. They'd actually want me to sit with them in the stands and watch the classes. I'd be sitting with my mommy and daddy, watching my girl friends out of the corner of my eye run around having the time of their life. They'd ask, "Why did that horse win?" or "Explain what makes a good show horse?" or other stupid questions. I'd roll my eyes thinking my parents were imbeciles for not knowing these obvious answers.

Finally, my poor mom and dad gave up and let me ride with the Cowarts to the horse shows. At first they drove an old truck that had just one working door. When we'd stop for gas everyone would pile out the passenger side so Mr Cowart could pump the gas and pay the attendant.

The radio didn't work, so Mrs Cowart would read us books or tell stories about showing in the early days with Love and Franny and the boys.

"You girls may think this truck is bad," she told us, "but when we first took our kids to a horse show we borrowed a garbage truck to transport the horses.

"They showed up at the Alabama state fair in a garbage truck full of horses and rabbit cages. At that time a horse show was held at the same time as the state fair. Mike was an enthusiastic student of breeding. He practiced this knowledge on rabbits, culling his breeding stock ruthlessly. 'I'm breeding the best with the best and hoping for the best,' he'd quote our friend Bob Smith who gave us Rex. Mike ran back and forth between the horse show and rabbit show checking on the progress of both.

"Love and her friend Debbie Denny led yearlings in the halter class. Peter somehow got his hands on a fire extinguisher and shot off a white cloud at them as they entered the ring. Love's colt threw back his head, flagged his tail and bounced his way to first place. Mike rode next and took third on Lad O' Shea, who was just a colt then, but later went on to become a World's Champion five-gaited horse.

"Mike put up his colt and ran to the rabbit show. All day he went back and forth bringing blue ribbons for several of his bunnies, but at the end of the day he came back with a surprise. A huge golden trophy floated along unsteadily toward our garbage truck where we were waiting for him so we could take the horses home. It looked as though it sprouted legs and was walking by itself. From its base these appendages clad in riding breeches took unsteady steps. I knew those legs," she laughed.

"Mike could hardly see around the trophy it was so big. His little buck had edged out all the hundreds of rabbits in the show for the highest honor. Mike sold him on the spot for an enormous sum of money – $40!"

I can't remember if the door on that old truck we rode in used to work before "the incident" or not.

On the farm, Katy and I got to do things earlier than other kids our age – like driving. At one show when I was thirteen or fourteen, Mr Cowart asked Katy or me to bring him the truck. Or maybe we volunteered to get it for him.

Anyhow, we raced to it. I won, so I drove.

"Press in the brake to start it," Katy instructed.

"I know. I'm not stupid." I was feeling rather grown up and wanted to impress the kids from the other barns. I turned the key until it ground going k-k-k-k.

"Stop turning the key! The engine's running already," Katy shouted.

"I know. I'm not stupid." I glanced at her frostily out of the corner of my eye. I hated backseat drivers.

I pulled the gearshift down on the steering column to D for drive and inched forward.

"You're not going to make it!" Katy warned.

"I know what I'm doing! I'm not stupid." I would too make it through those two trees. They weren't that close together. It would just be tight though – I'd have to squeeze. "Vroom," the truck sounded as I applied gas and brake at the same time, inching forward.

Then the noise changed to "Vroom, waaaaa," as the wheels spun. I applied more gas. I knew we could make it through.

"Stop! Stop!" Katy screamed. "Put it in reverse."

"I know! I'm not stupid," I said, feeling pretty stupid. But the truck wouldn't go in reverse either. It was firmly lodged between the trees.

"Oh no!" All of a sudden I had to go to the bathroom. My stomach felt like a large fist was squeezing it. "What am I going to say?"

About that time I saw the stout figure of Mr Cowart walking toward me. His bushy gray eyebrows were raised in surprise and his mouth was an O of astonishment. He walked up and leaned in the window.

"What do we have here?" he asked, as calm as can be.

"I thought I could squeeze through," I confessed around a stone in my throat feeling my face grow hot and red.

"Trucks don't squeeze," he said smirking. There was a twinkle in his eye and his dimples deepened. His shoulders started shaking, I could tell he was trying hard not to laugh.

I think I would have felt better if he had taken a riding crop and whipped me.

The announcers at the small shows had the most appalling Southern accents and often mispronounced our horses' names regularly. Jane Newton, who Mr Cowart teased as "the little rich Mt Brook girl," rode a giant of a horse named Charlemagne. He was as majestic as his namesake, the conqueror of old, standing about eighteen hands to his withers. Jane looked as tiny as a Barbie doll astride him.

The horses lined up after they had finished the class. They "parked," which means they stepped forward with their front legs keeping their back hooves planted. Their eyes were wide, almost white rimmed, and ears perked. The judge then walked around each mount for one final look and marked his card with first place, second and so on. It was an exciting time to wait for your name to be called.

Jane looked elegant, her dark hair coiled neatly in a bun, crowned by a sleek black top hat. Her tuxedo was tailored perfectly to her thin curves, gloved hands held high, keeping Charlemagne's neck arched in a perfect bow. All the riders, including Jane, looked across the fence at their horse trainers who said, "You did good. You should be the winner," to each of their protégés. But there could be only one winner, one blue ribbon, one silver platter – and everybody wanted it.

Jane waited, hoping they'd call her horse's name. It was a magnificent name for a magnificent horse, Charlemagne, the conqueror. Finally the judge handed his card to the announcer who, after a long pause, called out, "And the winner of the three-gaited class is ... Charles a Magnee or is it Charles a Manegee? Charles a Mangy ridden by Jane Newton! Come on over here, hon, and get yore platter."

Jane trotted boldly up to the winner's circle. They clipped the blue ribbon on Charlemagne's bridle. Jane kept trying to correct the announcer, "Shar-le-mane, his name is pronounced Shar-le-mane! Not Charles a Mangy!"

The photographer snapped a picture then nodded to the announcer.

"Take your victory lap Miss Newton!" he said. "There's our winner, Charles a Mangy!"

The organ music blared a rollicking tune as Jane trotted around the ring one more time, blue ribbon fluttering off Charlemagne's bridle. The whole way she shouted, "Shar-le-mane! His name is Shar-le-mane!"

Our show kit was a special suit for showing different kinds of horses. The pleasure and five-gaited riders wore tailored suits with long tails that swept back gracefully as they rode. The pants came down over the boot and were held in place by spats. Because of the matching tie that went with the outfit, I learned to execute a handsome Windsor knot by the age of twelve. Our long hair was twisted into a bun, held in place with a hairnet and a thousand pins. A matching derby topped it.

Three-gaited horses, also called walk-trot, sport roached manes. The riders wear tuxedos and top hats. These horses are elegant with lots of action, meaning their knees practically knock their chins when they trot and canter. With heads held high, their necks arch like swans.

Clothes weren't as formal when the Cowarts first started going to horse shows with their kids. Richard wore his Sunday suit, which consisted of a red plaid coat with black pants. Mr Cowart bought a paper bowler hat at the joke and magic shop downtown for the boys to show in.

When Peter Cowart was about ten years old he entered his first show. His older brother Mike thought it would be funny to enter him as "Howard Coward." It didn't matter that Peter won the class when the judge called his name as Howard Coward; he jumped off his horse and ran after his brothers with clenched fists.

The pleasure class back then had horses of different breeds, from Saddlebred to Quarter horse to mutts. Now the pleasure horses have as much action as the three-gaited horses, meaning they are high stepping and animated.

Saddlebreds are supposed to be jumpy and high strung. Mr Cowart ensured this by shooting bottle rockets at us when we worked out in the ring. The horses would enter the class on the verge of exploding. They'd snort, sounding like the air brakes on a semi-truck, with wide white-rimmed eyes. A walk was exaggerated, almost a slow jog. It was a thrill to control these loaded kegs of dynamite with the slightest pressure of leg or touch of fingers on the double reins.

Katy rode Mrs Cowart's horse, Willy, in several horse shows.

We'd arrive early in the morning and be there till late at night with the in-between hours full of a mixture of fun, boredom and sometimes sheer terror. At one show, to pass time, Katy rode Willy and I rode Jericho bareback around the gypsy camp of horse trailers. We were on the hunt for cute boys, or at least I was.

The show-horse coats were glossy and slick as oil so it was very slippery riding bareback in jodhpurs. Already jittery with so many stimuli around them, our horses shied, jumping sideways at every shadow. This made Katy and me slip dangerously, clutching their manes for dear life. As we rode along, the announcer called over the PA system for the Arabian costume class to warm up.

The costume class was a wondrous site to behold. The Arabians were decked out in colorful silks, looking like a cross between Lawrence of Arabia and medieval knights. Several of the horses wore silver bells that jingled when they cantered, sounding like Santa's tiny reindeer.

The rider's were dressed for the harem with scarves covering their faces and little else. They wore gauzy pants with matching bra tops. Many looked like frustrated housewives who had read one too many romance novels. But "It only takes a spark to get a fire a going," as the song goes and those Arabian-costumed freaks were the sparks that set off our two kegs of dynamite into wild fire status.

Out of self-preservation Katy and I jumped off our mounts and held them – unsuccessfully – as they snorted and wheeled in terror of the costumed ghouls that billowed past.

It all happened so suddenly. Everyone who saw it said it was a miracle.

I had always believed I was going to die young. Whenever something bad happened, I thought, "This is it, come get me Lord." I should have died then. But Jesus promised in the Bible, "No one can snatch you out of my hands." I guess he had his hands around me that day.

Willy leapt in front of Jericho and unleashed a mighty kick. Horses often kick each other and nothing happens, except maybe flattened ears and a bite in return. However, the power behind it can be devastating if it is delivered with intensity and hits a vulnerable area.

The costumed Arabians terrorized Willy and Jericho. Willy kicked, I guess out of self-preservation. Perhaps it was intended for Jericho, but it missed him altogether. A well-placed kick can do great damage if it catches a vulnerable spot. And to everyone's horror it caught the most vulnerable spot possible. Her hoof caught me squarely in the center of my face. I was lifted off the ground and sent sprawling on my back.

Stunned, I stared into the sky. It was a cool blue with cumulus clouds stacked like mounds of cotton balls. I looked carefully to see if Jesus was going to reach an arm down to jerk me up to heaven. But all I saw was a giant white rabbit standing upright. His two ears extended longer and longer as the wind pulled at the clouds like Play-Doh. They got so long that the bunny became a horse with a long swan-like neck. I wondered if I'd ride horses in heaven.

The horse morphed into another cloud creature when the worried face of Mr Cowart blocked the sky. His hair looked a little whiter, and his demeanor more frantic than it had been when I tried to squeeze his truck between the trees. How did he always manage to be there when I needed help?

Several other faces joined him, circling above me, blocking out the sky completely.

"I thought she'd be dead," I heard one man say. "Horse kicked me five years ago and I've still got a hole in my leg."

"Got her right in the face," one woman whispered. "I saw it with my own two eyes. I'm surprised anything's left."

"Are you okay, Mary?" Mr Cowart asked drowning out the buzz of vultures looking for blood. His thick, calloused fingers felt my face for internal injuries.

"I thind my dose is broke," I said as he felt it. "Dis makes dree."

"Tree?" Mrs Cowart asked. Word travels quickly at horse shows. There's the telephone, the telegraph and the tell-a-neighbor. Almost instantaneously she had heard about a girl getting kicked in the head. She ran toward the commotion, knowing in her heart it was one of her girls. Hooking her arm around me, she took me back to the horse trailer as Mr Cowart rounded up Jericho.

"De first time I broke id was a powder puff football game, de second was diving into a shallow pool. Dis makes dree," I explained morosely.

"Oh," she said with empathy, "this is the third time you've broken your nose. This makes three?"

I nodded gloomily. My nose had not stopped growing when my face had and the result was that people said, "You look like Barbara Streisand," which was a nice way of saying, "You really have a big nose."

One winter while skiing in Colorado, a lift operator saw me and said, "Wow! You look just like Golda Meier!"

This was a new name for me, so hoping she was some beautiful model, I asked, "Who is Golda Meier?" I batted my one asset, big blue eyes, and tried to look sexy, which is impossible in a giant white ski suit that made me look like the Michelin tire man. My nose was running and I could taste the salty snot on my upper lip.

The lift chair jerked against the back of my legs, causing me to plop ungracefully into it.

"She's the prime minister of Israel," he said, bringing the metal bar down in front of me with a clang. The lift whisked me away from my new admirer.

Somehow my imagination translated Jewish Prime Minister into "beautiful Jewish princess with large blue eyes – very glamorous." I told my friends, "The lift operator was flirting with me. He said I looked like a Jewish princess." I envisioned myself in one of the costumes the women wore in the Arabian costume class at the horse shows. Only I was much more svelte.

Only later did I find out who Golda Meier really was. I was glad it was much later.

My poor nose had a flat spot right in the bridge where a helmet had left its mark during that powder puff football game. Now this. To make matters worse, I had a red birthmark below my left nostril. It looked like the blood had left a stain there when I broke my nose.

The long weekend shows were a horse of a different color. We'd check into a hotel for several days, rooming with our best friends. It was a kid's dream come true. At first the Cowarts trusted us. They would say good night, and Jane, Nancy, Katy and I would close the door – for a little while.

We made friends with several kids from other barns and would sneak out after the Cowarts thought we were in the Land of Nod to swim in the pool or just run around the hotel. In Tuscaloosa we stayed in a high rise, which in Tuscaloosa is about five stories, but it had an elevator.

After Mr and Mrs Cowart retired we tiptoed out of our room and headed for the lobby. The kids from other barns didn't have as much supervision as we did, they would hang out together down there. We began a wild game of hide-and-go-seek slash tag. We dashed up the stairwells and raced on the elevators, forgetting that voices carry very well up stairwells and down elevator shafts.

Jane and Nancy raced down an elevator. When the first floor light lit and the doors opened with a ding, they got a rude surprise. An apparition wearing robe and slippers appeared looking very angry.

Mr Cowart stood and roared as the door opened, "Mary Lou Buck!"

For some inexplicable reason, whenever anything bad happened Mr Cowart always assumed I was behind it.

Jane and Nancy, to their great embarrassment, were escorted back to the room after a good chewing out. But warned by little birds, Katy and I hightailed it back and jumped in bed before they arrived. We were breathing heavily when Mr Cowart ushered them in, but our pretend snores didn't fool him.

That was the incident that led to the duct tape. Forever after, when we'd go to bed at night, Mr Cowart would duct tape our door so he would know if we'd escaped or not.

Every now and then Peter Cowart and Steve Willoughby would work at the horse shows. Peter was more interested in motorcycles and football than horses, but would come to the horse shows as a groom. Ironically, he would later become one of the greatest Saddlebred trainers in America. Steve was practically a member of the Cowart family. The Willoughbys lived on the next farm down Highway 119. They also had four kids who were all close in age to the Cowart crew. They grew up together as Mrs Willoughby said, "like a litter of puppies."

At the shows, Steve and Peter stayed busy all day washing horses, blacking their hooves with shoe polish, rubbing cornstarch into the horses' white socks. They brushed, fed and did whatever Mr Cowart commanded.

Back at the hotel we girls polished our tack until the silver stirrups shone like sterling. We'd use white shoe polish on the girths and oil the leather of the saddles and bridles.

Once we managed to get the guys' room key. While they were out working at the fair grounds we went in their room and turned everything upside down – mattresses, TV, lamps, suitcases, anything that could be moved. Chuckling at our cleverness, we went on to the competition.

Late that night we returned exhausted and ready to collapse into bed. We trudged along the outside balcony to our room, put the key in our door and turned the lock. The door swung open and Jane reached inside to flip on the lights. Nothing happened. "Shoot the light's burnt out," she said. Although it was dark inside, the outside light shone a dim pathway into the room.

For some odd reason we all felt slightly nervous but ventured in anyway. The room was completely empty. The beds were gone – mattress, box springs and frame – the desk along with the TV that sat on it.

Our suitcases – gone.

Shower curtain – gone.

Towels – gone.

Even the toilet paper roll was gone.

Jane began to hyperventilate.

"Oh, my gosh! Oh, my gosh! Oh, my gosh!" she repeated like a skipping CD.

We were in a state of shock. Someone had broken in and stolen everything!

We couldn't call the police as the phone was gone. We stood in the empty box of a room and stared at the four walls. "We've got to report this," Jane the oldest by one year became the adult in charge. As we started out to find Mr Cowart, Katy noticed something.

"Hey look," Katy said. Her index finger, which was double-jointed and shaped like a U, pointed at the window of the room next to ours. It was Steve and Peter's room.

"What, Katy," Jane said, irritated that we were stopping.

"What is it?" I echoed, looking toward the spot where Katy's finger pointed. The curtains were closed and I couldn't see anything but their white folds.

"Look down there. Don't you see it?" Katy asked.

"That's my blue suitcase!" Jane said in a high-pitched whine. Below the line of curtains we saw a jumble of clothes. Using the key we had procured earlier that day, we opened the boys' door.

All the contents of our hotel room were piled up to the ceiling. We could hardly even walk in.

"Oh, my gosh!!" Jane began her mantra again.

Playing Possum

*L*ove and Franny's riding experience was extensive. The Cowarts were turning out many young horses and had over forty-five in their stable when Love was around twelve years old. Lad O' Shea was her favorite colt, he was so hot – filled with anticipation to go – he was difficult to ride. Franny would hold him as near the fence as possible, then Love would leap from the top rail to his back where he'd explode into action.

Love was elegant and graceful when she rode. Mrs Cowart thought her beauty was the perfect complement for the aristocratic elegance of American Saddlebred horses. "I'd get goose bumps when I watched her," she told us with tears in her eyes. "I was so proud of her that I just could hardly stand it."

But Franny and Love by no means abandoned their first loves, Madame and Boogaloo. After the show horses were put in the barn, the girls would mount their ponies bareback and head for the mountains.

When you say Alabama, people think, "Flat, hot, cotton fields, populated by uneducated, barefoot, prejudiced red-necks." However, Alabama is actually an Indian word meaning, "To clear the thicket."

Although Alabama does have its share of uneducated rednecks, in Mountain Brook, an affluent Birmingham suburb, folks not only wear shoes, they wear Prada. Mountain Brook is reportedly the sixth richest city in America. Don't quote me on this. I'm just quoting some other unnamed person.

The Great Smoky Mountains prop their feet in rolling waves across the northern half of the state. When someone from Alabama says, "Lets hike up Oak Mountain," someone from out west might say, "Where's a mountain?" But our beloved foothills are mountains to us.

Katy and I too loved the "mountain trails." We got there by exiting the Cowart's driveway, crossing Highway 119, and meandering up rural roads past farms and shacks to old dirt roads. A persimmon tree hung invitingly over a fence along the way, tempting the uneducated to take and eat.

Katy first made the mistake of trying a persimmon because I convinced her they were a rare delicacy, seldom found in uncultivated gardens. Which is true of the large variety, but the little ones are nasty.

"The Emperor of China had several imported for his garden from Europe," I said, without the slightest compunction about lying through my teeth. "They're best when they're hard, like an apple. When they get soft they're rotten." Several soft ones littered the ground, paying tribute to my deception.

Poor Katy chose a hard persimmon and I watched with wicked fascination as her cheeks sunk deeper and deeper into her face in a good impression of a dehydrated fish. She spit and sputtered using the horse's mane in an effort to wipe the bitter taste from her tongue. After that she considered it her duty to get any new person who rode with us to try the "delicious fruit from China."

An unassuming dirt logging-road that forked off the country lane was our "yellow brick road" to miles and miles of trails that zigzagged their way across Double Oak Mountain.

Whenever we didn't know what to do next we'd ask ourselves, "What would Love and Franny do?" We became connoisseurs of Love and Franny "isms," things we were sure they had said or done but having no earthly idea whether they had or not. If one of us said, "Well, they did it," it would be gospel. You could push your personal agenda through with a declaration that it had originated with them.

I'd tell Mr Cowart, "Me and Katy are going to the mountain trails," to which he would whack us with a riding crop, "Katy and I, not me and Katy." He was ever-diligent that we wouldn't grow up talking like rednecks.

"Schools don't teach English like they used to. One day it will be obsolete and everyone will say, 'me and him went here' or 'ain't it right, Bubba!'" He'd shake his head and we'd hear him muttering, "What are those schools teaching?" as he sent us off with our paper-bag lunches.

A peanut butter and jelly sandwich with an apple was the Power Bar of the day. It fueled us for exploring the mountain trails all day in search for Chimney Rock. When Love and her buddies rode all day long they tied their sandwich bags with hay string to their ponies manes. Katy and I poked the end of the bag into our back pocket where it flopped against the horses' rears as we trotted along.

Peanut butter never tasted so good as it did after it's been wrapped around an apple for several hours in a hot bag. At school Katy and I would try to mash our sandwiches around apples, but it was never the same.

Once we took our favorite teacher to the mountain trails for a ride. She brought her boyfriend for moral support, which goes to show Miss Green was no dummy. After all, we had been the terrors of the playground. We rode ahead of them and hid in a thicket. When they came walking slowly by, moments later, we jumped out yelling, "Yaaaa!"

I don't recall their horses getting scared, but we scared Miss Green so badly she fell off and started crying. I always wondered later if Katy and I were the reason her boyfriend broke up with her.

In the winter, as we trotted up the trail, the curb chains on the bridle would ching, ching, ching like silver bells. The bare trees stretched their naked arms up, silently mourning their stripped glory and begging God to return and restore them to their true state. They looked cold and angular, shivering in the frigid wind. Every sound was sharper in the winter. It seemed like you could hear a mile away.

"Crack!" we heard gunfire in the distance.

"Do you think the hunters will shoot us?" Katy asked. The week before, her namesake, Kathryn, a pretty little chestnut filly, had been shot and killed by hunters. They had crossed the fence and wandered through the woods onto Heathermoor Farm property. I guess they needed glasses, because they mistook the foal for a deer.

"Hunters are so stupid," Katy remarked viscously. "I'd like to shoot them."

"They shoot anything that moves," I said feeling my stomach tingle with fear of bullets whizzing by. "We've got on orange hats and coats, surely they won't shoot us."

"They'll prob'ly shoot the horses out from under us, thinking we're riding a deer," Katy said gloomily.

"Billy told me to sing really loud and they'll leave you alone," I quoted my brother often. He was my hero.

"Sing what?"

Ching, ching, ching went the curb chains, as if requesting a song. "How 'bout Jingle Bells."

It was one song to which we both knew all the words, so we belted out, "Dashing through the snow, in a one horse open sleigh, hey, hey, hey. O'er the hills we go, ho, ho, ho, laughing all the way. Ha, ha, ha."

We came to the top of the first ridge and looked out over the valley. In our imaginations, hunters crouched behind every bush. We turned tail and ran all the way back to the farm.

Invisible pins and needles jabbed our feet as we jumped off feeling as if they shattered into ice crystals. We pulled off the horse's bridles and turned them loose before hobbling into the house. We made hot chocolate and went to thaw by the fire that always blazed merrily in the fireplace during the winter. We sat at Mrs Cowart's feet.

"Tell us a story," we chorused with our backsides to the fire till our pants got so warm they felt like hot coals burned our buns. At that point we'd turn and thaw the other side.

"Whenever Franny came to visit Love," Mrs Cowart began, "she brought her pony, Boogaloo, along with her bird – in a cage – and sometimes her Irish Setter. I can still see them." She smiled at the long ago memory.

"Franny would arrive in the dusky evening. Instead of unloading her pony in the usual way, she'd climb in the back of the horse trailer, birdcage in hand, and slip her leg over Boogaloo. With one hand holding the birdcage, she'd push the halter from the pony's head. Boogaloo would half-back and half-leap from the trailer," Mrs Cowart slapped one hand past the other. "Like a shot! They'd be off, bridleless, with Boogaloo running like a wild Indian pony. Franny held the birdcage in one hand, her other flung out wide felt the wind wash over it in waves. The dogs yapped at the pony's heels as Boogaloo thundered toward the house. Franny would yell, 'Here I am, everybody!'

"The Willoughbys from two farms down had four kids too. We met them the day Love fell through the chimney. Mrs Willoughby took in Peter, Richard and Mike so we could stay with Love in the hospital. It was an odd way for them to get to know each other.

"Their oldest son, Steve, is the same age as Richard, and their next son, Doug, had a twin sister. They were the same age as Peter. Peter and Doug would go 'hunting.' That is they'd shoot cans, squirrels and sometimes horses.

"What!" Katy and I were horrified.

Mrs Cowart laughed, bringing a hand up to push the hair from her eyes, "Only dead ones," Mrs Cowart's eyes twinkled.

Did that really make a difference I wondered.

"One afternoon in the hot summer," Mrs Cowart continued, "Peter and Doug hit the woods to do some huntin'. Mr Cowart heard them across the river shooting. 'Bang, bang, bang, bang.' Gunshots went off one after another like popcorn.

"It turns out they had been shooting the carcass of a horse that had recently died. Mr Cowart had gotten Peter to drag it to the horse graveyard, with the tractor, but evidently Peter neglected to bury it. Instead he used it for a spot of target practice.

"Mr Cowart had an idea of what they were doing so he met them by the bridge and said, 'Peter, go get the tractor and get that dead horse. We're being sued for wrongful death. The vet is coming out to do an autopsy.'

"Peter and Doug's eyes about popped out of their heads. They turned and took off running. Peter knew his daddy would wear him out since that horse was riddled with bullets!" She laughed heartily along with Katy and me. We were rolling on the floor.

"The Willoughbys' oldest daughter, Debra, was Mike's age, but she became Love's close friend. She looked like Heidi, with long braids hanging like thick golden ropes over her shoulders. In high school she won all the beauty awards.

"Debra's pony, Cream Puff, was a gelding. The girls laughed at his sissy name. He and Debra looked alike since they both had long white bangs hanging in their eyes. Cream Puff wouldn't stay at Heathermoor with Madame and Boogaloo.

"Debra's pony, Cream Puff, was a silver-gray Shetland with white mane and tail. But Cream Puff was no cream puff.

He was equally as self-assured as his mistress. However, as long as Debra was on him his will bowed to hers, which was stronger. But when subjected to ropes, fences or barns his stout heart overcame them all. He'd jump through the window of stall doors. Doorknobs fit his mouth perfectly. Distance was no problem, either. His homing instincts were flawless. Every morning while the other ponies had obediently submitted to fences and stalls, Cream Puff was back home in the Willoughby barn inside the gate and fence!"

"The girls would try to shut Cream Puff up in the barn at night so they could all ride together the next day – or sooner. I didn't find out till later," she added as a side note, "the girls would sneak out at night."

"Sneak out at night!" Katy and I had to hear about that. Franny told me how she and Love snuck out at her house in Mt Brook, but I'd never heard about them sneaking out on the farm.

"I'm amazed that Mr Cowart and I were so naive to the girls' nighttime activities," she said. "Many nights Love, Franny and Debra climbed out the window, caught their ponies and rode away. They'd ride out toward the mountain trails and run through people's yards shouting, 'The Red Coats are coming the Red Coats are coming.' When the lights flashed on in the houses they'd gallop away into the cover of darkness. Of course, this ruined the girls' efforts to evangelize them when they'd ride by during the day and put Christian tracts in those same people's mailboxes.

"Sometimes in the middle of the night they would lie down in the middle of Highway 119 just to feel the warmth of the pavement against their faces and bare feet.

"Their biggest delight was the freedom of enjoying things forbidden by propriety in the daytime and being free from adult interference.

"Love never told me," she smiled wistfully. "It all came out bit by bit over time from Franny and Debra. Franny told me how much she enjoyed growing up out in the country with Love. It taught her things she never could have learned growing up in the city.

"Once Franny found a dead possum in the road. She jumped off Boogaloo and picked it up by its tail and tried to scare Love and Debra with it. When she laid it to rest on the side of the road and hopped back on Boogaloo, Debra called, 'Look ya'll!' The possum was scampering away into the shadows. There's so many country sayings people use but don't know the backgrounds. That episode gave Franny a real-life re-enactment of the meaning of playing possum."

When summer rolled around, Katy and I were determined to go back to the mountain trails and find Chimney Rock. Love and Franny had gone there, according to legend, and we would find it too.

We found Hidden Lake, which was as the name implies, a lake in the middle of nowhere waiting for us to discover it. The place seemed enchanted because we had to ride through overgrown sandy trails, which suddenly opened into a clearing. However, it was never as much fun to ride there alone.

When I was with Katy or Nancy I thought the lake looked magical and inviting, as if water nymphs waited below the surface for us to come and play. We'd swim our horses across, holding onto their manes, drifting along beside them. With a group of three or four we'd play water polo if someone brought a tennis ball.

However, once I rode to the lake alone. It wasn't the same inviting place that welcomed my friends. It seemed sinister – a hiding place for monsters that would grab me and pull me under if I touched the water. Or maybe a maniac was hiding and waiting for me! Maniac is a scary word. The thought made me run in terror, glancing behind me all the way back to the barn.

Near the lake a rough road scaled the mountain at almost a ninety-degree angle. I always wondered how in the world it was made. I couldn't imagine any machine driving up that steep, rocky hillside. Katy and I virtually clung to our horses' manes for dear life, our bodies dangling back across the horses' tails as they scrambled straight up to the sky.

We never confirmed it with anyone but ourselves, but believed we'd found Chimney Rock. Once on top we tethered our horses to a tree where they stood blowing hard, glad for a rest. We climbed the remaining boulders to the pinnacle and pounded our chests shouting, "Er-e-er-e-er" like Peter Pan when he done something worth crowing about. As if we had really done anything but hang on for dear life! Our horses looked at each other, scoffing in disgust over our self-aggrandizement. But we fed them an apple and they were content to give us the glory.

We had accomplished another Love and Franny. We sat at the top and wondered, "What do you think they did when they got here? Do you think this is really Chimney Rock? Do you think they swam in Hidden Lake?"

The view was glorious. We shaded our eyes and looked into the valley. We imagined we saw Mr Cowart staring back at us with binoculars. You could barely make out the white barn. It looked like a toy from this height and distance. On the other side of the ridge was forest as far as you could see, turning into a blue green haze at the horizon.

These roads would have been a dangerous place to be injured. We were miles from any farm or house and it was way before the invention of cellphones.

One time a group of us girls had been out in the mountain trails all day and decided to canter along a long, flat stretch of road. Unexpectedly, our horses hearkened back to when their ancestors raced on the track, or at least possibly a great uncle. Each as if on signal took its bit firmly between their teeth and ran flat out as if wildcats were after them. We went from fun canter, to an exhilarating gallop, to a heart-stopping nightmare in a matter of seconds.

When something like that happens you never can be sure what your horse will do. It might miss a turn, bolt through the trees and leave its rider decapitated by a low branch. It could step in a hole and go down, breaking a leg and your neck in the process. Or it could simply slow down and stop.

It's easy to panic, not knowing which way you will die.

I can't remember the circumstances, why she lost her seat, but in the middle of the pack Katy started to slip sideways.

It was noisy. In the thunder of the hoofbeats and the shhing of wind blasting in our ears, I'm not sure what if anything was said. I just remember seeing Katy slipping in slow motion, inch by inch over the side of her horse. I wanted to reach over and grab her. I remember trying. I might have yelled, "Grab my hand Kat!" Her eyes were wide and frightened. She reached up, but the "thudup tup tup, thudup tup tup" of the horses' beating hooves were like a magnet pulling her under. She disappeared under the mass of horses. She was trampled.

I didn't know till much later how hurt she really was. Katy was too tough to tell anyone about her injuries, even her parents. Like Love she was very private, so she suffered in silence.

The Sheep Who Thinks He's a Dog

*L*ife wasn't all fun and games for the Cowart offspring at Heathermoor. They all shared the responsibility of running the farm. Early in the morning before school the boys made the trek to the barn. Mike did the feeding and haying of the barn horses and Richard fed the pasture horses. Peter did the long, boring drudgery of watering. In the evening after football practice they'd repeat the process.

Love's chore was washing dishes. "When I grow up I'm going to use paper plates," she growled as water sloshed up wetting the front of her shirt. "Better yet! I'll marry a rich man and just throw away the dirty dishes." She threw the napkins in the trashcan to punctuate her point.

She complained every night, "Why do the boys get to feed the horses? It's not fair!"

Finally, going behind her parents' back, she had a powwow with her two older brothers. "I'll do both your jobs – feed the inside and outside horses – if you'll take the kitchen."

Richard and Mike readily agreed to swap jobs. But they wanted to make sure she didn't take it back. "No whining and moaning when you have to get up every morning," Richard warned.

"No take backs," Love assured them. "I'm just as strong as ya'll and can do the job better and quicker than both of you put together."

The next morning Richard and Mike laughed and splashed water as they tossed the dishes. One washed and the other dried and stacked.

Mr Cowart walked through the kitchen, "Hey, boys," he said. Then something clicked in his mind. He stopped abruptly, doing a double take. "Hey, Boys!" he practically shouted. "There's no way you could be done with the feeding yet. What are you doing up here? Where's Love? "

Richard turned around, "Whoa, Daddy. One question at a time."

Mike kept his back to his dad, continuing to wash the dishes. He'd let Richard talk his way out of this one.

"Love wanted to change places..."

Mr Cowart cut him short, veins popping out on his neck, "You boys made your little sister do your work!" he roared.

"No! No! Listen Daddy," Richard started again, backing up. He held his hands out placating, "Love wanted..."

"Love wanted? I think you and Mike wanted. You wanted to get out of your jobs!" he thundered. "Love's just a baby! She can't do that kind of work."

"Baby, nothin', she's thirteen years old!" Richard shouted throwing the towel down.

"That is a baby!" Mr Cowart boomed back.

Enter the peacemaker.

Mrs Cowart hated confrontations. "Stop yelling, both of you! John, you know Love's been complaining about the dishes and begging to trade chores with the boys. I'm sure all this was at her instigation. If she's so bent on women's liberation, let her be liberated a few days. I think she's the one who needs to see how hard it really is to feed forty-five horses."

Mr Cowart was devoted to his little girl. He was like a big bull with a ring in its nose that she could lead around wherever she wanted. He turned on his wife, "But Love..."

His expression reflected the struggle of hopelessness. "She's ... she's ... this is ridiculous. She can't do that kind of work!"

"Let Love make that decision," Mrs Cowart reasoned. "She won't die from a little hard work."

Meanwhile at the barn, Love, with the help of her little brother, Peter, was loading the feed into the wheelbarrow to roll it around to each stall. It was still dark outside because the days were at their shortest. She and Peter huffed. Their breath came in small puffs like white phantoms that mingled then disappeared as they lifted the heavy bags.

"This is what I was made for!" Love thrilled. "Finally I get away from the ball and chain of dishes, dishes, dishes." She threw a handful of sweet feed in the air to celebrate.

Peter didn't say a word. He just kept his head down, no doubt wondering how long her elation would last.

After school that afternoon Love hopped in the farm truck with Peter and drove to the barn to do the evening feeding. "High-five, Peter! This is awesome. No dishes tonight, yeah, yeah, yeah!" Driving was no big deal, even for a thirteen year old. She'd been driving through the pastures ever since her feet could reach the pedals.

"See ya. Wouldn't want to be ya!" Love pointed at Mike and Richard, dropped her napkin on the dinner plate, and jived out of the kitchen. "I'm likin' this. Oh yeah. Uh huh, uh huh."

Mike and Richard rolled their eyes and began clearing the table.

The next morning as Love walked out the back door Peter climbed out his window and tiptoed across the patio roof. Benny, the sheep, walked around the corner and looked up at him, mouth watering. Or at least Peter thought its mouth watered.

"You can't get me up here, you little savage," Peter said and grabbed the nearest tree branch. He shimmied across it to the trunk. Benny, on the ground, followed his progress never taking his eyes off Peter. Love started the pickup. She opened the gate, drove through, closed it and then drove along the other side of the fence.

Peter had begun to edge out onto a branch on the other side of the tree trunk, one that hung out over the fence into the pasture.

When Love got under it she stopped. Peter lowered himself till he hung directly over the truck bed. He dropped in with a thud and banged twice on the roof. Love zoomed down through the pasture with Peter in the back, thumbing his nose at Benny.

Benny was a sheep. He used to be such a sweet little sheep – a gift from a neighbor. Mr and Mrs Cowart had put the nappy-headed little lamb in bed with Mike. The little Suffolk baaaa'd, waking him. The sleepy-eyed boy was thrilled to find this real-life stuffed toy in bed with him.

The dogs had sniffed Benny all over at first and then settled back down in a pile napping with him. After that, Benny seemed to think he was a dog. When the dogs rushed out to bark at a cow, or to greet a new face, Benny rushed with them. When the dogs flopped out panting on the patio, Benny knelt beside them chewing his cud. He even followed them on their hunting sprees.

The first time Benny went hunting, the dogs came back without him. Mike and Love worried about him and spread out over the farm to search for the lost lamb. After looking everywhere they enlisted their parents' help.

Mrs Cowart searched along the Little Cahaba. It was getting dark and she was about to give up when a bleat sounded above the rushing water. Looking across the river she saw a little white head poking out of the foamy water.

Benny didn't move a muscle. Only his eyes followed her as she waded out to rescue him. He was precariously perched on a large submerged rock. Otherwise he would have drowned. "You crazy coot," Mrs Cowart chided as she lifted him in her arms, "how'd you get out here?"

She carried him up to the barn where there was great rejoicing over the lamb that was lost, now found. "Mamma, you're like Jesus, saving lost lambs," Love crowed.

Benny wasn't dumb as most sheep. Even though he still hunted with the dogs, he never got left again. Maybe the dogs had pushed him in as an initiation.

However, if Benny thought he was a dog, Peter thought he was a ram. He would get down on hands and knees and butt heads with the lamb, teasing him unmercifully. "Dumb ole sheep," he'd say, "Baaa, baaa, I'm gonna get you." Whack! He'd smack his curly black head on the white woolly spot between Benny's eyes.

It didn't take too much of this teasing to awaken the sleeping instinct in Benny that whispered, "You're not a dog; you're a sheep. And not just any sheep, you're a ram!"

Benny began to grow little horns, which he began to regularly test on Peter. Finally, it seemed his one goal in life was no longer to be a dog, but to settle scores with Peter. Benny grew a lot faster than a nine-year-old boy, and he was developing his punch. He'd flatten his ears against his head, roll his eyes around a time or two, drop his head and rear off the ground before colliding like an All-American tackle with his target. He could knock a child Peter's size flat.

That's why Peter had to sneak out his window and climb through the trees to do his morning watering.

Since Benny seemed to have eyes only for Peter, Love could stroll out and get the truck to pick him up.

The nights grew colder as winter progressed. One morning Love and Peter found they couldn't turn on the water at the barn. Love went to the phone in the office and rang the house. "Daddy, the water won't turn on." Peter stood beside her, hugging himself and hopping from foot to foot in a futile effort to keep warm. "Pipes frozen! What do we do now? Do what?" she shrieked into the receiver.

"What? What?" Peter tried to grab the phone out of her hands.

Love snatched it out of his reach, "But Daddy, that will take forever."

With their parents' help, Love and Peter had to haul water in fifty-gallon drums from the house to the barn in the back of the pickup truck.

"Slow down, Momma!" Love shrieked, "It's all sloshing out."

"I'm creeping like a snail," Mrs Cowart called, "it's going to spill. There's nothing we can do about it."

That night Love didn't make any comments as Mike and Richard took her plate to wash it. She just sat in her chair, staring bleary-eyed.

Mr Cowart wanted to end it there and then, but Mrs Cowart urged him to wait, "Let it be Love's decision, or she'll blame you for making her quit."

It didn't take long. After another week Love was exhausted. It killed Mr Cowart to watch her drag around. She would have quit sooner if she hadn't been so stubborn.

Grudgingly she learned to respect her older brothers' masculine capabilities. She looked at her calloused, red hands one night after dinner, swallowed her pride and said, "Okay y'all, I'm sorry. I just can't do it anymore. Can we trade back jobs?"

"No take backs!" Richard said. "You wanted to trade, we've traded. I'm likin' this dish job. You said you could do my job quicker and better. Well I can do this job quicker and better."

Mike just looked down at his plate and smiled. He was a man of few words, but when he spoke it was usually something profound. He was content to let everyone else battle it out.

Mr Cowart slammed his fist on the table, rattling the silverware and making the water jump in the glasses. With one look he silenced Richard who knew better than to argue with his daddy about who was going to do what. He'd enjoyed the hiatus from the hard work, but the vacation was over.

One afternoon when Love had finished working the horses she walked slowly back to the house. She was tired and glad she didn't have to stay and feed them. "I'll never complain about doing the dishes again," she said to herself.

As she neared the house she noticed Benny the ram. He had been stalking Peter but turned his head and stared at her. She froze, staring back. He flattened his ears and rolled his eyes preparing to charge.

Love picked up a heavy board lying by the fence. As Benny came at her with his head low for the kill, Love swung the two-by-four like a pinch-hitter in the World Series. It slammed him backward and fractured one of his little horns.

Benny stood, stunned, legs spread, shaking his head. He looked at Love with new respect. After that he never bothered her again. As far as he was concerned she was the alpha sheep. He went back to Peter as his number one prey.

But the relative peace didn't last long. Although he never charged anybody bigger than Peter, when friends came with small children it wouldn't be long before Benny materialized out of thin air. They'd find him standing arrogantly over a shrieking, flattened child.

Peter put him to good use. He used his "battering ram" to settle accounts with his enemies by luring them into Benny's range. One smart-alec kid that Peter disliked got his tooth knocked out by Benny on the front porch, much to Peter's delight. Another particularly bitter enemy found himself locked in a stall with the ram.

However, Peter couldn't outwit the sheep every time. One afternoon he snuck out through the garage to ride his bike to get the mail. Pushing the bicycle stealthily, he scanned the horizon. The coast looked clear. Benny must be on the other side of the house. Gingerly he threw his leg over the bar and began pedaling down the long white drive to the road.

Clackety, clackety, clackety. Peter's blood froze at the sound of the little hooves galloping behind him. Pedal, pedal, pedal, pedal! He began pushing the gears as fast as he could make his legs spin. Clackety, clackety, clackety, the sound grew louder. If only he could make it to the tree! He put on a burst of speed.

The race wasn't even close. The seventy-pound ram quickly outstripped his opponent.

Bang! Pow!

Almost simultaneously the ram bent the fender and blew out the tire. It was time for Benny to leave Heathermoor.

Years later it was reported that only one large man with a two-by-four could go into the field with Benny. I'm sure Love could have gone too.

Camp Lumberjack

At thirteen Love had caught – as Mrs Cowart put it – "a virus that shattered her natural reserve.

"Like a rabid dog, she was driven by a wild compulsion she couldn't seem to control. It manifested itself in her leaping through the air, contorting her limbs, and shouting loud, silly rhymes. Not only was Love afflicted, the virus affected most of her friends. It didn't matter what their physical shape or athletic ability, the normally sane girls, seemingly for no reason at all, any time or place, would all begin leaping and shrieking, veritably foaming at the mouth. Even the most inhibited seemed to cast aside all restraint whenever the compulsion took them."

The cheerleading virus attacks pre- to mid-teen girls every summer. Because Love made the cheer squad the first year, Mr and Mrs Cowart got to watch their three oldest children perform at the same time every

Friday night. From the bleachers they'd cheer for Mike and Richard on the gridiron, and watch Love flail arms and legs on the side lines yelling her lungs out, "Go Briarwood!"

The Cowart children attended Briarwood Christian School. Along with the Willoughbys and Debbie Dennie, they all piled into the Chevy Impala on school days and carpooled the fifteen miles in to school. In those days there were no seat belts and they all piled on top of each other. When they arrived, other kids at school stared in amazement. It looked as if they were in some kind of contest to see how many people you can stuff into a car at one time.

The first year the school fielded a football team my brother, Billy, suggested a name for their mascot, the "Hairy Armadillos." Their coach, Pete McKenzie, had been a professional baseball player. He coached the junior high boys only two weeks before their first game.

Briarwood's apprehensive yet eager young boys met Highlands Day School on their field. The opposing team had been playing together since early grammar school. Not only that, some of them looked like they had been shaving for a couple of years. Billy swears he saw some of the so-called junior high boys driving their own cars to the game. "They must have been held back," was my mother's response. The Highlands Day team towered over the Briarwood boys. The Hairy Armadillos resembled their namesake, small and timid.

The next year they changed the mascot to the "Fighting Lions," hoping to inspire more awe in their adversaries.

Richard Cowart had always been easygoing and seemed somewhat lazy. But on the football field his star began to shine. Mrs Cowart concluded he had rested all his life saving up energy to expend it on the football field. He hit his opponents so hard he cracked his helmet. They had to order a special one just for him. This made him easy to spot. His black one stood out in the field of golden helmets.

The next year as cheerleading try-outs took place for the ninth grade, Mr and Mrs Cowart assumed their daughter would be one of the girls in short skirts again. However, the judging was different from the previous year.

Briarwood Christian School was affiliated with the church that Frank Barker, their brother-in-law, had started. It was fairly new and the teachers and administrators tried hard to found everything they did on prayer and seeking God's will in the Bible.

Since the Bible is a little vague on cheerleading the judges met together before the try-outs to pray and ask God for wisdom to mark their cards fairly.

The Friday afternoon after cheerleading try-outs, Mrs Cowart walked from the barn up the gravel road to the house. She met Love and Franny driving in the opposite direction to the barn.

The truck slowed to a stop and Love leaned out the car window, resting her chin on her slender arm. She looked up at her mom with soulful, brown eyes rimmed in red. She had stopped wearing her glasses the year before because her lazy eye had perked up and decided to tow the line.

Love hated emotion. In serious matters she almost seemed untouchable.

"There's nothing more painful than watching your child suffer," Mrs Cowart later told me. She ached for Love, seeing the unwelcome tears gather.

"I didn't make the squad, Momma," she stated briefly, batting the tears away before they had the chance to form lines. Turning her face back to the road, she straightened and drove on to the barn.

A storm of emotions rolled over Mrs Cowart. She learned that Love was the only girl from the previous cheerleading squad to be dropped. Mr Cowart thundered that he'd go wring the judges' necks. The darling of his life had been wounded, and that was inexcusable.

Angrily Mrs Cowart drove to see Briarwood's principal. Sally Dewberry hid behind the judges' decision. They had scored on a points system. Love missed out by one point.

"The judges scored everyone on a very impersonal system," she said. "They honestly believed God had guided their decisions. Don't you think as Christians we need to believe God has a purpose in this?"

When he heard Mrs Dewberry's explanation, Mr Cowart fumed, "It's easy for her to sit there and say, 'God's will this and God's will that.'" He thought people at the school often pushed their own way by claiming it as God's will. "Does God really care who's a cheerleader and who isn't? That's the silliest thing that spineless, skinny woman has said yet!"

Several of the teachers believed it silly too. They banded together to overrule the judges' decision. Love met one of them in the locker room the next day. "Love, we're going to overrule the judges' decision. You are one of the best cheerleaders this school has. We're not going to let them spiritualize this mistake." She gave Love a warm hug.

Love submitted to the embrace for a moment, then pulled back. "Miss Gumby," she said, voice trembling, "I appreciate your concern. But I know why I didn't make the cheer squad this year."

It was Miss Gumby's turn to back up. She stared at Love in confusion, "What do you mean, Hon?"

"I know this decision is from God. I had let cheering become an idol in my life. It was all I cared about. Also I'd become quite a snob."

Love didn't like sharing her heart. But she didn't want the teachers to overrule the judges' decision. She wrote in her diary, "I understand that my relationship with God will last forever. It has eternal value. I don't want my relationship with him to suffer because of *anything* else, even if it means 'cutting off my right hand.' Plus, I don't want to be a snob."

With the fall weather that cooled everything down came the football season. Love still enjoyed the games and sat in the stands cheering with the crowd for her brothers and boy friends. Though she was too young to date, her parents let groups of boys and girls come out to the farm and "hang out."

One weekend the girls and the boys decided to have a camp out.

When they were younger, before they had become boy conscious, the Cowarts let them all sleep together at the camping spot they had developed across the river.

Under the trees close to the river was a clearing, Camp Lumberjack. It had been frequented so often no weeds or sticks littered the area, which was smooth, hard-packed dirt. Large white rocks circled the charred cinders in the fire pit from previous camp outs. The boys kept split firewood in huge stacks around the edges, marking the boundaries.

Now that the children were teenagers their parents let them "hang out" all they wanted during daylight hours, but at bedtime boys and girls had to sleep in separate spots.

The girls slept in the Willoughbys' barn, and the boys would be at Camp Lumberjack. They thought since it was across the river, through the woods, with a mile and a half of fields and barbed wire fences between them it would keep them separated.

However, when there's a will, there's a way.

Around 11 p.m. John Willoughby drove up the Cowarts' driveway. Seeing a light on he knocked on the kitchen door. Mr and Mrs Cowart were just getting ready for bed, confident that everything was under control.

"Where are the boys?" Mr Willoughby asked without preamble.

Mr and Mrs Cowart looked at each other then looked at their neighbor. "They're settled in across the river," Mrs Cowart answered. "We haven't heard a word from them."

"Well," said Mr Willoughby, "I think they're at my house."

Mr Cowart loved a good fight. He wanted to catch those boys red-handed and whip them all the way back across the river to where they belonged. "Come on, let's get 'em," he said, rubbing his hands together and grinning.

He and Mr Willoughby chuckled the whole way back to the Willoughbys' farm about catching the boys and scaring them to death. Upon entering the Willoughbys' driveway they turned out the headlights and coasted to the gate. They carefully closed the car doors with a muffled click and tiptoed to the barn. They heard giggling.

Mr Cowart put his finger to his lips and gestured that he would go in the front while Mr Willoughby circled round the back to catch the boys as they tried to escape. Mr Cowart climbed the ladder to the loft and shoved the door open with a bang, "Got ya!" he shouted.

Every girl squealed with one voice.

"Daddy!" Love shouted, slightly embarrassed and proud. She had the opinion that her dad was pretty cool, but he was still a parent and they are forbidden at slumber parties.

"Where are the boys?" Mr Cowart demanded, walking through the isles of sleeping bags and kicking at the hay. "Come on out you rascals!"

He couldn't get anything out of the girls except giggles.

"What's going on here?" he demanded.

"Nothing!" Franny snickered.

That was all the explanation he got. He backed down the hayloft calling, "John! Did you catch any of them?"

Mr Willoughby had been equally unsuccessful. They looked at each other suddenly, each thinking the same thought. Camp Lumberjack! They raced to the car.

Back down Highway 119 they drove, gunning the car as they sped back up the Cowarts' driveway. They bumped down the gravel road, through a field, and across the bridge. The car lights shone on the trees around the camp like a spotlight searching the prison yard. But the boys were sitting, calm as can be, in their sleeping bags, sipping hot chocolate.

Mr Cowart looked at his friend as if to say, "You dragged me out at this time of night for this?"

"I know I heard something, John," Mr Willoughby defended himself. "Those boys had to have been at my place."

The two men drove back to the Cowarts' house discussing the situation. "There is no way those boys could have run a mile and a half, over barbed wire, through the fields, across fences, through the woods, over the river and been back sipping cocoa in the time it took us to fly back in the car." Mr Cowart rattled off the obstacles in a pepper of machine-gun word bullets. "Everybody knows that rubber on the wheel is faster than rubber on the heel. They can run pretty fast, but not fast as a car."

Mr Willoughby conceded that he could have made a mistake. He dropped off Mr Cowart and headed back to stand guard over the girls.

If they had only looked a little closer they would have seen the pulse pumping in their throats and heard their hearts thudding like Indian war drums.

When Mr Willoughby had been attracted to the barn by the giggling girls, the boys had raced across the road to the little Mount Hebron Church on the hill overlooking the Willoughbys' brick house. An old cemetery with a quaint wrought-iron arch over the entrance stretched out on the hill behind and to the left of the church.

Hiding among the tombstones the boys watched Mr Willoughby drive away to the Cowarts' house. It was dark and spooky crouching behind the stones on top of dead men's graves. Visions of haunts and spooks filled their imaginations, making them want to get out of there as quickly as possible. But something else scared them even worse.

"Ker-POW!" a shotgun exploded nearby. "I see you boys!" a voice yelled from the parish house. "Ker-POW!" the gun shot again. "You better git out of here, you vandals, or I'll git you!"

He didn't have to ask twice. The boys raced out of that graveyard. Like buckshot from the gun they scattered, running headlong back across the fields as the crow flies toward Camp Lumberjack.

Doug Willoughby and Peter Cowart were slower than the older boys and were left behind as the others' adrenaline carried them over fences, river and woods at warp speed. Doug went down as he leapt a fence, then falling to his knees he grabbed Peter and started pleading, "Pray Peter! We've got to pray! Right now! Lord, save us! Merciful God, spare our lives!" He shouted at the sky. He thought he'd been shot in the rear. But it was only a barbed wire puncture from the fence he'd jumped.

"Ka-boom!" the gun sounded one last time. God answered his prayers by giving them a surge of adrenaline to get them back just before their daddies showed up.

Not to be outdone, the girls hiked down the side of the highway to get the boys back later that night. Headlights shone in the distance as they trudged down the side of the road. "Everybody huddle together and act like a rock," Love the dramatist suggested. The girls piled together, holding very still, sure they looked like a large rock. Evidently the car thought so too, because it sped on by without slowing.

When the girls arrived at Camp Lumberjack they crept forward through the trees like a group of commandos. "Don't make a sound till you see the whites of their eyes," Franny instructed.

At Franny's signal the girls jumped out like Gideon surprising the Midianites. "Yaa!" they screamed.

The boys just looked up bored. "We heard ya'll a long time ago. You're about as quiet as a herd of elephants."

"Sure you did, that's why Doug wet his pants."

"I didn't wet my pants when you yelled," Doug protested. "I wet them when the preacher shot at us."

Franny surveyed the camp for food supplies. "Man, your camp stinks," she said. Cooking was half the fun of camping. "All you have is a pack of wieners. I guess that's fitting, since you're just a bunch of wieners."

"That's because all girls do is eat. We boys do more manly things," Richard said in defense.

"Like what?"

"We light our farts," Peter snickered.

Raiding the boys' camp was so anticlimactic the girls headed back home. Halfway back they were met by Mr

Willoughby driving frantically back to Heathermoor Farm. He wasn't fooled by their rock impersonation.

Camp outs were hard on daddies.

Franny introduced Katy and me to Camp Lumberjack. She showed us the sacred spot, explaining how to set the metal grill over the burning wood to cook.

We planned our first camp out with much anticipation. Nancy, Katy, Jane and I planned our meals out as carefully as we packed our things. Having the world's largest sweet tooth, all I wanted was s'mores – graham crackers with a Hershey's chocolate bar, topped with toasted marshmallows. After you ate one you always want s'more, hence their name.

Mr Cowart loaded our gear in the back of the truck. It piled up high as the cab. We girls rode our horses and ponies behind the truck in a festive parade to the campground. After tethering our horses to nearby trees we went to help Mr Cowart unload our junk.

We rolled out sleeping bags and prayed it wouldn't rain. Tents were for sissies. Mr Cowart used his lighter to get the fire going and made sure we had enough wood. The Cowart boys had grown up and no longer stocked the woodpile at Camp Lumberjack. The place was now deeded to the next generation. It was our job to take care of such details.

Twilight was upon us and the sun's rays were just a memory on the land. Lightning bugs winked through the trees. Nancy caught one, pinched off its glowing bottom and pressed it to her earlobe. "Look, earrings!"

"Ewww," Jane stuck out her tongue, "that's a bug butt you've stuck to yourself."

"Ain't it cute," Nancy came closer to Jane. "Here, you want it." She stuck her finger in Jane's face. It was loaded with the offensive glowing bug guts.

"Stop! Nancy," Jane squealed and jumped over sleeping bags to get away. "Get that nasty thing out of here!"

We settled in to cowboy beans and s'mores while Nancy told ghost stories. Everything was dark and spooky. Crickets chirped and night birds called. A whippoorwill sang his distinctive "Whippoorwill, whippoorwill," to which the Bob White answered, "Bob white, bob white." The stars winked through the trees as the wind stirred their branches.

This was freedom! Away from parents, adults and social propriety. We could do whatever we wanted.

Jane fell asleep as soon as it got dark, but Katy, Nancy and I sat up yawning and determined to have some fun. The summer days were long and we were exhausted by the time the dark finally came out to play.

"Let's go for a night ride," I said. "We have to. That's what Love and Franny would do. Think about it. It's like tradition or something."

Katy looked out through the dark trees. But what about the man with the hook who tried to murder those girls in their car? Nancy, you said they never found him. What if he's here?"

"Nancy, you should never have told that dumb ole' story!" I said, giving her a shove. "If he's here we can outrun him better on the horses!"

We all looked through the trees as if searching for ghouls. Jane slept peacefully, oblivious to the danger.

The three of us bolted for the horses. I grabbed a bridle and shoved the bit between reluctant teeth. Swinging up we galloped away, leaving Jane to her fate.

The cool night air was refreshing and we soon forgot the ghost stories and enjoyed the thrill riding in the dark. Out in the open pasture it wasn't as gloomy as it had been at Camp Lumberjack. Although the moon was waning, stars punctuated the ebony sky like the millions of angels carrying tiny candles. As we lay back on our horses' rumps we looked up at the galaxy. Their coats radiated heat and kept us warm. We began pointing out familiar constellations.

"Look there's the Big Dipper," I said, pointing at three stars in a row with two above on the outside.

"That's not the Big Dipper, dummy," Nancy corrected, "that's Orion. The three stars are his belt. Look, the Big Dipper's over there." She pointed out the big, four square with the long ladle.

"Oohh! I saw a shooting star!" Katy squealed.

I had never seen a shooting star before. At home my dad built a platform on our roof for stargazing. At night sometimes the whole family climbed a ladder with blankets and pillows. Mom, Dad, Billy and I would snuggle together. Everyone but me would see a shooting star. "Over there!" Billy would point. But as soon as I looked it would have burnt out. I began to think they were making it up.

However, Heathermoor, as I said before, was a place where dreams came true. That night the stars fell on Alabama. It must have been a meteor shower because we saw about a hundred fall from the heavens. God gave us a laser light show we never forgot.

We passed over the bridge and rode toward the barn. It was dark as pitch, but some of the horses inside heard us and Hmmmmed a greeting.

As we looked up the quarter-mile of sloping pasture, we saw a few lights twinkling from the windows of the Cowarts' house. It looked secure and handsome, sprawled elegantly across the crest of the hill. The elms were like great giants standing guard, holding their wide black arms over the house protectively.

We turned back and looked across the river. The trees over there didn't look like they stretched out their arms for protection. They looked more like the ones from the Wizard of Oz when they tried to catch Dorothy and Toto. We sat for a moment glancing first at the house then back toward

Camp Lumberjack. We came to a silent but unanimous decision. As one we galloped up the hill.

Tumbling through the kitchen door, we trooped into the living room where Mrs Cowart was curled on the couch reading her Bible. She smiled when she saw us and patted the cushions for us to join her.

We hadn't been there long when we heard the kitchen door slam. Jane stumbled in. "You mean things! I can't believe you left me!"

Closed Doors

*L*ove's bedroom door still vibrated from the violence with which Love slammed it. "What happened to my sweet little girl?" Mr Cowart wondered.

He had just informed her she couldn't go out on a date with a boy driving until she was fifteen. "And that's still too soon," he grumbled to himself, not looking forward to the day when some boy took his baby girl away.

At fourteen and a half Love had hit adolescence. Her usual sweet disposition had disappeared under eye-rolling and complaints about rules and restrictions. Although Mr Cowart could get through to Love at times because she considered him cool and strong, Mrs Cowart felt more and more alienated from her teenage daughter.

Little did they know their silent child was penning her life's secrets and struggles on reams of farm stationery and notebook paper. Although she didn't share her feelings with her mom or dad, she was transparent with them as she wrote to her heavenly Father.

"I want to please my God and be close to Him and worship His wonderful majesty," she wrote. "I want to be humble before Him, yet be His devoted friend. I want to learn the secret of a happy life, but I want to learn it *now* while I'm still young."

She was beginning to fall in love with one of her older brother's friends and the thought of him consumed her. "Love is a pretty word – It's my name – that makes me feel special. People don't forget me, because my name is Love, and I should 'love' people and make them 'love' me. Lots of people love me. Jesus loves me, my parents love me, Franny loves me, Aunt Barbara loves me. Maybe someday 'he' will love me," she wrote on Heathermoor farm stationery, April 7.

At fourteen Katy and I had eyes for Peter Cowart. The dark curls that hung over his large brown eyes made him have to lift his chin to see you. It was a "Hey, baby" look that made all the girls swoon. He was the starting quarterback for the football team a couple years older than I was. I began to experiment with makeup hoping he would notice me. But it probably just made me look like Bozo the clown.

Katy brought her family's trampoline to the Cowarts' house and set it up by the back patio. After riding showhorses all day we'd come up for lunch and jump.

Peter happened to be home one afternoon and came out the back door as Katy and I were jumping on the tramp. Be still my beating heart! We three had a blast double-jumping each other – one person jumps just before the other lands. This catapults them into the air. When Peter double-jumped you you flew up to the branches of the elms. I was so in love.

After awhile, we sat down to cool off. I was laughing and talking, hoping to gain Peter's attention. I did. But not in the way I hoped.

He looked at me and screwed up his face. "Pew! Mary! You stink like a field hand."

I guess I needed a hit of Teen Spirit.

Love didn't have any problem attracting the opposite sex. At fourteen she was lithe and, let's just say, nicely developed. Looking closer to sixteen, she left a slew of broken hearts in her wake. Yet she only had eyes for one guy.

She wrote in her diary, "I've set many goals that have become a part of me. I want to be an actress, a writer, and a leader in one of many areas, to be famous and change the world. I want never to forget to take life easy and relax and love. I'm only conscious of 'him' and God, all the time. 'He's' part of my conscious now, just like God."

But her beloved wasn't ready to return her feelings and their relationship melted like snow in the spring. Love was heartbroken.

Because she never revealed secrets to her parents, they only saw the outward signs of an inward struggle. Love called home from school one day saying she was sick. Mrs Cowart picked her up around lunchtime.

"What's the matter, Love?" Mrs Cowart asked as Love slammed the car door and slumped in the front seat.

"I just don't feel good," she mumbled, turning her face to look out the passenger window.

Mrs Cowart bit a fingernail and looked at her daughter out of the corner of her eye.

"Say something, say something," she whispered to herself. Her mind was blank. *How can I get Love to open up? Why am I afraid of my own children? This is ridiculous,* she thought as she reached to feel her daughter's forehead, but Love shoved her hand back and snapped, "Don't touch me, I don't have a temperature."

Realizing she was sick in the deepest sense – sick at heart – Mrs Cowart asked, "Do you want to tell me what happened?" Silence. "What kind of mother am I if my only daughter won't confide in me?" she wanted to say. Instead she just stared straight ahead as they drove home in silence.

Love went straight to her room shutting the door with a resounding slam. "Why are you building a wall between us?" Mrs Cowart whispered as she stared at the door wishing she could break it down.

Love wrote, "May 4, Five minutes ago the thought of being cheerful and courageous at school tomorrow seemed impossible, but I found this verse: 'Keep up your courage and let us show strength for the sake of our people' (at school don't be moody or depressed) 'and for the cities of our God.' (Maybe I'm being a stumbling-block to some other people.) 'Then let the Lord do what is good in His sight.' It's up to Him. I've dedicated our relationship to Him. This is about the hardest thing I've ever done. I'm crying at the thought of losing 'him,' but 'he's' God's now. I've given 'him' to God. It's up to God whether He wants to give 'him' back. "

As the days progressed, Love began to look upward instead of inward. On May 6, she wrote, "Dear God, I decided that You are going to be the most important thing in my life. What's 'he' compared to You – ZERO! God, I'm also surrendering all my rights to You: the right to date, to love, to be hurt, to talk about people, to be happy. Everything. I mean business. God, help me keep these promises."

May 29, "I guess the Lord wants me to find comfort in Him, I wish he'd send me some comfort in the form of something human. Maybe when I learn to depend on Him to fulfill all my needs, He'll give 'you' back to me. I feel like this is real love because I don't demand anything in return."

June 15, "The one thing that's come out of all this is I think I have a pretty good grasp on the idea of what love is.

"Love is: 1. Patient – put up with his shortcomings, don't let them bother me.

"2. Kind – I should be kind to him always, thinking of making him happy.

"3. Loyal – never say or do anything to hurt him.

"4. Believe in him and defend him – I should expect good of him and let him know it. Let him know I have confidence.

"5. Not jealous.

"6. Not selfish – always think about what's best for him.

"7. Not rude.

"8. Not boastful.

"9. Not irritable.

"Love isn't based on reason, or it wouldn't be love – it will forgive and put up with faults on either side.

"I don't ever want to be jealous. I don't want to cut people or gossip. I want Him to be proud of me; the way I look, the way I act, the way I dress. I want to be sympathetic and sweet and friendly to everybody. I just want Him to be proud of me" (Colossians 3). "Most of all, let love guide your life.

"Right now I'm learning to relax and enjoy life. I'm *convinced* that's the secret to life. Don't get uptight. Right now, I'm proud to be a Christian; I'm not ashamed at all. I'm even ready to face persecution.

"Maybe I don't love 'him.' Maybe God just let me think so, so I'd learn this lesson I'm learning. Good night!"

Mr Cowart seemed to be able to roll with the punches and even deliver a few himself since he could still beat the boys in wrestling matches. But Mrs Cowart felt alienated by her children.

"Why, God!" she'd cry out. "Why can I no longer see your light shining through my children? I know I've made mistakes, but no one has tried harder to be a good parent. I've taught them the Bible, loved them, stayed home with them, prayed for them and with them, tried to lead them in the truth by example. We've sacrificed to send them to a Christian school. What more can I do?"

A promise from the Bible echoed in the back of her mind, "Raise up a child in the way he should go and when he is old he will not depart from it."

"But God!" she cried, "I don't want to wait till I'm an old lady! I want to see the light again now!"

"What do you *really* want for your children?" a masculine voice came from nowhere.

Mrs Cowart turned around. One of the dogs, Buddy, wagged his tail. It thump, thumped against the ground and his pink tongue lolled out in a smile. She looked carefully at him then shook her head. Buddy hadn't spoken like Balaam's donkey. "Was that you, Lord?" she asked. "Did you speak to me? You know I want my kids to belong to you."

A flood of thoughts ran through her mind about her true desires for her children. Did she want God's light to shine through them so they would be more understanding of her, their mother, or so she could enjoy having "fellowship" with them?

A new realization came to her. Even if she had the best relationship with her kids; if they had the best health, beautiful clothes, all the material possessions they thought they needed; if she gave them the best education so they'd be the most successful businessmen, scientists, artists, athletes or whatever, in the end, which comes to all men, when all these things have vanished away, they will have ultimately gained nothing and lost everything.

The only thing she could ever give her children that would last, or be of any real value in this life, or in the one to come, is a relationship with God through his Son, Jesus.

She shared this paradigm shift with her husband. Mr Cowart, in his own private way, had been struggling with the same questions and come to the same conclusion. As they prayed together the next morning they both cried out to God, "Lord, all we want for them is YOU! Let them fulfill the one reason for which they were created – to know you, understand who you are, believe what you say and bring you glory through their lives. Whatever it takes – our lives, their lives, anything Lord – let them glorify you no matter what the cost."

Later Mrs Cowart wondered if she would have prayed that way if she had known what that cost would be.

Raft in the Pond

When I arrived early one morning at the barn I grabbed the first horse I came to in the field. All the trail horses were free game. Everyone shared. If someone wasn't riding, you were free to use their horse.

Big was Catherine Hare's horse. His name wasn't original, but it was accurate. He was a great big bay mongrel of no distinct breed. But he was a great trail horse and easy to catch.

His breath was hot and pungent from the sweet feed he was still munching. The bit clunked over his long yellow teeth, and bits of corn and oats dribbled onto my hand, hot and foamy. I wiped the sludge on my jeans, threw the reins over his head and grabbed a hunk of his black mane to swing up.

It was a hot day and soon the sweat from his back soaked into my jeans making them cling to my legs. I cantered to the gate of the front pasture and looked over at the pond.

Something floated in it, but the tree limbs blocked my view and I couldn't tell what it was.

Holding onto Big's thick neck, I leaned down and undid the chain that fastened the gate. It clanged as it dropped and the hinges groaned when it opened. I bumped through it still on Big's back. I hated getting off if I didn't have to, but mares and foals were in the front pasture that time of year, so I had to hop off and relock the gate before I could investigate the pond.

As I trotted down between the old apple trees I saw an inflatable yellow boat floating in the center of the brown water. Hands and feet dangled over the sides.

"Where in the world did you get that thing?" I yelled.

Katy's head popped up, sunglasses shading her eyes giving her the illusion of sophistication. "I found it in our garage this morning. I had to pump it up at the gas station."

The big yellow boat did its best to look nautical, but it belonged on the ocean instead of this wet-weather pond. The end of the long rope that encircled it disappeared into the murk of the dirty water.

It didn't take much encouragement for Big to go into the pond. He gladly waded in until water swirled around his withers. He snorted at the strange yellow beast that carried the girl and he didn't want to get too near.

"I'm trying to get some sun. I've been so white from living in my blue jeans all spring," Katy said, as she applied more Johnson's baby oil to her already greasy arms. No self-respecting teenager used sun block back then. We generously oiled our limbs to entice the sun to singe us, the bronzer the better.

"I'm the one that needs sunglasses! Your legs are so white they're blinding me." I made a grab for her glasses, but Big lunged sideways. He couldn't move too fast, weighted down by the water surrounding us, although his bulk caused a wave that sloshed over the side of Katy's lifeboat.

"Quit splashing!" Katy scooped her hand along the surface to get me back. I tried to return the favor, but Big kept moving and I had to keep turning around. Katy was gaining the upper hand so I sat on him backward for a better splashing position.

Big began to dunk his nose and blow bubbles. Then he pawed with his front legs. He enjoyed it as much as we did. I swam him across the pond once, holding onto his mane and gliding beside him so I wouldn't weigh him down. The water felt good but looked disgusting with bits of mud and other unknown brown and green sludge floating around me. I'm sure my mother wouldn't approve, but that's what made it so much fun.

"Give me that rope," I called as Big swam past the raft. "I'll take you on a ride."

Holding the rope attached to the raft, I pulled the little rubber dinghy around behind me as Big swam. The drag of the raft was too heavy for me to hold onto for long. The rope kept slipping from my grasp and I'd have to swim Big around to grab it again.

At this point one of us got our great idea. I guess we should have known better. Mr Cowart certainly thought we should have. Even now, looking back, I wonder how I was to know that little stunt almost cost me my life. At the time we thought it was better than jet skis.

"Hey," I said, "I'll tie the rope around Big's neck and then I won't keep dropping it."

With the rope firmly knotted around the horse's thick neck Katy surfed behind the wake of Big's churning hindquarters. I'm surprised our whoops of delight didn't arouse suspicion from the house as it was around lunchtime.

I always hoped for great things – like maybe some hunky boys would see two beautiful girls in bikinis, at least one in a bikini and one in soggy blue jeans. They would be overcome with our beauty, run through the field to us and beg for kisses – or at least ask us on a date.

At times like that I was the beauty in the Coca Cola commercials, laughing and having the time of my life. It didn't take much for imagination to fly me from reality to raptures. In reality, I probably smelled worse than a wet dog.

My beautiful blonde hair had the texture of steel wool. I tried to brush it but it was so thick the brush bristles could only penetrate so far into its mass. The top would

look relatively smooth, but underneath a mass of dread-
locks. When the horses' manes were tangled Mrs Cowart
would say the witches had been riding them in the night.
I wondered if they tangled my hair while I slept.

Katy took a few turns around the pond riding high and
waving to the imaginary crowd from her chariot like a prom
queen in a parade. When Big stopped swimming the raft
drifted up beside him and we decided to change places.

Forgetting his aversion to the scary monster raft, I pulled
Katy up close to make the exchange easier for her to leap
onto the horse and me into the raft. Big's snort sounded
like a truck tire had blown out on Highway 119. I felt every
muscle in his powerful body contract before he exploded.
He reared back then lunged forward as if the raft had grown
fangs and was going to eat him.

On land this could have been enough to throw me to the
moon, but with the water up to his neck it only felt like a
violent lunge. But it turbo thrust on our pool toy. I hate to
sound like a sadist, but it was funny watching Big's eyes turn
white and his nostrils red with fright. This became our new
game, "scare the horse and ride the rocket raft."

I guess at that point we should have known better, but
hindsight is 20/20.

After several of these rocket rides Big changed his
strategy. I guess he decided once and for all to get away from
the terrible tormenters who subjected him to raft torture.

He reared straight up, front legs breaking the surface of the water. Time stood still. The wind stopped blowing, the crickets stopped chirping and I stopped breathing because I knew he was going to fall over backward.

I'm usually a quick thinker and normally would have jumped out of the way, but there was one thing stopping me – the rope.

When Big finally back-dived on top of me the rope wrapped around me, pinning me between his powerful legs and the raft. I knew I had to get away from this mad machine we created. I felt Big's legs thrusting and churning the water, pummeling my body. I was kicking just as hard to get out of the noose that had hanged me.

Katy had backflipped out of the raft by the impact of Big's fall. When she surfaced she scanned the pond but didn't see me anywhere. "Mary! Mary!" she screamed. All she saw was the horse speeding across the pond to the opposite shore. The raft followed jauntily behind, but there was no other sign of life.

She began to swim and dive, searching the mucky water for my body, which she was sure was smashed into the bottom of the pond. "Help! Help! Somebody Help!" she yelled, then dove to feel for my body.

No one was near. The cars whizzed by on the highway oblivious to the drama below. The Cowarts were in the house on top of the hill and couldn't hear. No one could help. She turned her face to the sky and cried, "Lord! Help me!"

She wished that she and I had never written those Love-copycat letters saying we were going to die young. It had sounded romantic at the time to be called to heaven by God. But when death was at the door the intrigue vanished.

Big neared the shore and I was still nowhere to be seen. A fist of fear squeezed Katy's stomach. She thought she might throw up. Her throat tightened as hot tears poured down her wet cheeks. She launched into the stroke she used at Leeds Country Club as lifeguard. She had to get help. Remembering the story of the colt that was taken by this same pond she retched. She had to get out of this place of death.

Suddenly the water exploded ahead of her. She screamed, envisioning skeletons and ghouls. Gasping and coughing, I surfaced.

I sucked in air, lungs burning.

Katy sprinted to me and grabbed me in the headlock lifesaving maneuver. "Mary! Mary! Relax. I'll get you out of here. Are you okay! What happened?"

For moments I could only gasp and cough and try to get the mud out of my eyes. I tried to ward her off. The water was shallow enough to stand.

To this day I can't explain what happened. One moment I was bound and the next I was free. Did the same angels who had watched over the man whose car crashed under the bridge save me too?

Big reached land and began a strange dance with the raft that was still attached to his neck by the rope. To his horror the beast actually followed him out of the lake. Like the creature from the Black Lagoon, it just kept coming.

He froze, trembling all over, and glanced back nervously. The raft stopped too. He took a timid step, but the raft also moved forward. He stopped again looking straight ahead. He probably hoped if he ignored it it would just go away. He took another trembling step and looked back; to his horror the raft inched up behind him.

If stealth didn't work he'd try force. He kicked it viciously and was terrified when it exploded in a "Pow!"

That did it. Big took off like a shot from a rifle, running madly through the field over rocks and logs. Then that big old horse gathered all his strength and sailed over the gate snapping the rope that attached the monster to him. It was the first and only time we ever saw him jump – the raft, deflated, crumpled and twisted on the fence post.

I trembled all over. "I think I'm going to be sick," I said, imagining my body broken and wrapped around the gate with the raft. There was no way to explain my release from the tangled lines. Rope burns ran completely around my legs. I looked toward the bridge and thanked God for what must have been his angels looking after me.

Mr Cowart heard the commotion. He appeared at the fence by the secret garden. When he saw Katy supporting me up as we trudged up the hill, he knew there'd been trouble. We forgot our fear and had started laughing as we recounted the spectacle of Big's fear of the raft, but down deep we were shaken.

Mr Cowart didn't laugh. I think he would have liked to horsewhip me with the riding crop in his hand if I hadn't bean beat up already.

"You girls have got to use your heads! That's the dumbest thing I've ever heard. I can't believe you tied that rope to that horse's neck!" As he fussed he slapped his leg with the crop to emphasize each word. "That's the dumbest," whack! "thing," whack! "you've ever done," whack, whack, whack.

Every stroke was a nail in my head hammering a reminder of the letter I had written and hidden saying I was going to die young. It was always in the back of my head. Would I die young since I had written it? Did I really want to? When would it happen?

It's the
Hormones, Honey

They say things get worse before they get better. But who are the "they" that say it? Love was becoming a raging teenager. She complained about everything her mother asked her to do.

Quotes from the book of Job in her diary reflected the inward turmoil that manifested itself outwardly to her parents. "Oh, that my sadness and troubles were weighed. They are heavier than the sands of the seashores. I am weary of living. Let me complain freely. I will say to God, 'Don't just condemn me, tell me why you are doing it."

"Love, you're such a drama queen," Debra Willoughby would say. "One minute you're in the throws of ecstasy and the next the pits of despair."

In the book *Fried Green Tomatoes*, Mrs Threadgood said, "It's the hormones, Honey." That was her explanation of why her friend was going insane. She was going through "the change." Teenagers go through a similar change at puberty when they change into adults. "It's the hormones, Honey."

Love wrote, "I feel better, I read Ephesians chapter two about God's mercy. I've also learned that God is my strength and my true friend. I need not worry. I can rest all my problems on Him. He'll gladly bear them because He loves me."

Like most teenage girls Love was obsessed with clothes. She wrote in her diary, "I love clothes. I wish I was rich and had lots of cute clothes and a blue convertible MG, and I'd go shopping all the time, or I'd take my cousins places and go see people. I found two dresses I love (really three). I hope Daddy will let me buy them."

Love bought every product on the market to enhance her physical beauty. She had products to grow nails, curl eyelashes, whiten teeth, clear eyes, thicken hair, remove hair and clear skin. Her Daddy called them her "chemicals" and planned to buy her a dressing table for Christmas to store them all. He teased her mercilessly about having her ears pierced. "Why don't you just put a bone in your nose too?"

July arrived bringing fireworks and heat. Along with July came a change in Love. Her mom and dad noticed a remarkable transformation after she turned fifteen. She quit complaining about the dishes and asked her parents, "How can I help?"

Mrs Cowart wanted to shake her and ask, "What have you done with my real daughter, you alien being?"

She also noticed a wistful dreaminess about Love as if she saw something others couldn't. For the first time Love and her mom began to have the deep spiritual talks Mrs Cowart always longed for. She was amazed at the depth of wisdom her daughter had hidden inside.

Love willingly helped her mom tackle the tremendous mess of their attic closet. It was a thrill for Mrs Cowart to have her daughter so grown up and capable of helping her. She was a different person than she had been just one month before. Mrs Cowart wanted to throw her arms around Love and cry. She was elated with the commonplace little adventure, and afraid Love would think she was crazy if she knew.

Late in July Mr Cowart's father died. He loved his own children so much because his childhood had been one of upheaval and loss. His dad had divorced his mother when he was a little boy. She disappeared from his life and no one ever spoke her name again. When he had four children of his own he gave each of them his whole heart.

Love wrote of him in her diary. "We got up at 5:00 this morning to go to granddaddy's funeral. I met some of Daddy's relatives. They were all nice, fine people. Daddy didn't act sad. I don't think he was. He's such a wonderful, strong person. He's such a *man* in every sense of the word.

He *never* complains and *never* shows emotion. I don't see how anybody in the world can be as strong as he is. I think he's the most wonderful man in the world. Mamma's the luckiest person. God must really love her. I'm so afraid *my* husband won't be half as good as Daddy and I'll be disappointed in him. I guess God will give me the right person so I don't need to worry."

Love and Franny competed all summer in equitation. It is the art of riding, where the rider is judged for what they can make their mount do.

Love rode Lady B. Good, a grand old walk-trot mare, and Franny rode Denmark's Thunder. Showing the handsome horses, the two girls were the picture of elegance and grace in their tuxedos and top hats.

Love was outgrowing her first pony Madame. When she and Franny would ride out on the trails Love's legs practically dragged on the ground. A neighbor had a cream-colored pony who was larger and very sweet tempered – a welcome change from Madame. The pony's name was Heaven.

She and Franny looked forward to the most prestigious horse show of the season in Louisville, Kentucky, where the world champions of the Saddle Horse breed were crowned. They wouldn't be riding but would be there to watch the first-fruits of Heathermoor Farm's breeding program perform in the three-gaited stake for junior horses.

The great event is held at the Kentucky State Fair Grounds in the coliseum known as Freedom Hall. Here the elite of the Saddle Horse world gather from all over the country. The pageantry of "stake night," when the world's finest, most-tested three-gaited, five-gaited and harness horses meet to vie for the roses, is the most magical moment in a horseman's life. All the lights dim in the arena as the orchestra begin the strains of "My Old Kentucky Home."

Each contender bounded into the ring with the spotlight focused on him as the announcer called the names of horse, rider and owner. When the cast was complete those "peacocks of the horse world" would begin a display of motion, precision and elegance, directed by horsemanship of the highest degree.

To produce a horse of quality enough even to be in contention on stake night is a feat most people in the horse world never accomplish. The Cowarts' dreams of glory were pinned on Crystal Springs, an elegant chestnut mare, the first foal bred and foaled by the miracle stallion Rex.

Crystal had been nurtured and trained on Heathermoor Farm. Love had been her jockey and Mr Cowart had driven her to the cart. Doss Stanton, a talent scout in the horse world, had purchased her. He put her with the right trainer to prepare for this very night in Louisville.

Love, Franny and the Cowarts sat in a reserved section just above the box seats in the center of the coliseum. Love and Franny had dressed elegantly in formal evening gowns befitting the grand occasion. Love's dark hair hung over her champagne-colored dress in a soft wave. She held her head high and sat straight, watching with anticipation.

Looking at her daughter, Mrs Cowart felt like Love had grown up. She had left her silly teens behind along with her surly attitude. She had become a pleasure to her parents.

An intense air of excitement enveloped Freedom Hall. Around the ring metal plates were hung. Each bore the names of a particular year's winner of the five-gaited stake, projecting a glory from the past.

The bugle blew for the junior three-gaited stake and they waited expectantly. The first graceful young horse bounded into the ring, knees and hocks popping as if on springs, delicate ears on alert, and large expressive eyes bulging with fire and spirit. "There she is!" Mrs Cowart called.

"No, that's not her, momma," Love said, still straining to see the next horse coming behind. "There she is! Look! Here she comes!"

Love gripped her mother's hand and pointed. Crystal Springs radiated elegance with every springy stride; golden highlights glinted in her tawny coat.

Franny and the Cowarts were spellbound. "Wow." The one word summed up their collective feelings.

The horse's history passed through Mrs Cowart's mind... Love's fall, Rex's fall, Love's recovery along with Rex's,

Rex siring the colt, Rex dying, the brood mare giving birth to Rex's foal, halter-breaking and training. That bushy adolescent filly that Love had ridden was now the most gorgeous of all creatures! She felt as if her heart would burst with pride as she watched Crystal Springs perform. Slipping an arm around her daughter she felt Love sigh. She wondered if Love wished she were riding Crystal now.

When the workout was over, the class lined up. Riders dismounted and saddles were removed so the judge could fully appreciate each horse without the distraction of any equipment. He took his time walking in front, to the side and behind each horse. They were dark with sweat and steam rose from the heaving sides. Pink nostrils blew hard from their exertions.

Crystal stretched her long neck out with ears perked. Her eyes were wide with excitement. Love waved, "Over here, Crystal Springs!"

Franny, more aware of her surroundings, chided Love, "Calm down! Quit yelling."

Love settled back, praying silently for her horse to win.

After the horses were resaddled and riders up, the judge went to the center of the ring to mark his cards. Everyone waited on the edge of their seats.

The lights were dimmed and the spotlight shone on the announcer. Bum, bum, bum, bum, rolled the drum. The announcer shouted, "And the reserve world champion of

Come Away Beloved

*T*uesday, August 28 dawned dry and hot. School was only a week away and Love was anticipating it. She told Franny, "I'm excited about the football games and cold weather. Oh, it's fun. It's exciting! I can't wait." But later in the day she recorded in her diary, "I don't know why I feel so yuck. Somehow I feel the Lord feels sorry for me. I wonder if something terrible is going to happen to me?"

Franny had always gone to a different school than Love. She had grown up going to the prestigious girls' school, Brook Hills. Their separate lives at school didn't seem to matter when they were little. They were always close as sisters. However, as high school began, Love had developed closeness with some of her fellow cheerleaders that drove a little wedge into her friendship with Franny. It hurt Franny to see Love drift away from her and cling to these new friends.

The summer before tenth grade Love became the coach for the junior high cheerleaders. She chaffed over the possibility that some of the girls on the squad would not measure up to her idea of perfection. She knew she couldn't kick anyone out. That would hurt their feelings, and she knew what that felt like. She drilled them constantly to discipline them into a good team. Most of the time she was utterly frustrated, vowing never again to take that job.

On Thursday, August 30 Love prepared a devotional for her cheerleaders from a book that had been her constant companion of late. The title was *Come Away My Beloved*. She carried it everywhere till it was dog-eared from use. She even studied it in the tackroom between horses she was working.

At the meeting she told the younger girls, "The only safe place to be is in the center of God's will. I feel confident that I am in the center of His will right now. Because of that I have a feeling that something wonderful is going to happen tonight."

Love waited at school for football practice to end so Richard could take her home. She sat alone on the steps of the gym where someone snapped her picture sitting with her knees folded to her chest, chin cupped in her hand, waiting.

When Love turned fifteen, earlier in the summer, her daddy finally let her go out on dates. She had a date that night at 7:00. As soon as she got home from school she jumped into the shower to get ready. She came out in her shocking-pink robe to talk to her mother, who was watching a TV program about show horses.

Some younger girls who were heading out for an overnight at Camp Lumberjack stopped by the kitchen. "Love!" they begged, "Come join us when you get home. Please!"

"Maybe," she half promised. "I'm not sure what's going to happen. I may not be able to."

Franny had been at the barn and stopped by Love's room on her way home to a slumber party. She found her wearing a pale champagne-colored dress.

"Where are you going?" Franny asked laughing. "This isn't the Love I know. What's with the dress?"

"I put on my blue jeans..." Love pointed to the bed where her blue jeans lay crumpled in a pile. "...But, I changed my mind. I just feel like looking beautiful tonight." She began brushing her long, silky brown hair.

"Well, if that's what you wanted you achieved it." Franny hugged her friend. "I never saw you look more beautiful."

When Love came back to where her parents sat, Mr Cowart exclaimed, "Wow! I don't think I'll let you go tonight. You're too pretty. My little girl is all grown up."

"Oh, Daddy." Love kissed his cheek. She wandered into the kitchen, opened the fridge and grabbed some grapes. She gave her dad another hug as she went back to her room. In a few minutes she reappeared, this time in Franny's white organdy dress with tiny pink rosebuds. It was lovely, but a bit too short for her.

Mrs Cowart saw her coming from her bedroom, straight and slender in the soft white dress. The white contrasted dramatically with her olive skin and dark hair. Love was radiant. "This is what you'll look like as a bride on your wedding day," she said as Love came up to her.

Love went out leaving her Living Bible on the messy bed with her well-worn book, *Come Away My Beloved*. She entered a short notation in her diary, "I'm wearing a dress tonight – me! Can you believe it? I'm really excited about tonight!"

Her date arrived and she said goodbye to her parents. Some of the girls who rode at the barn were still there. She whispered to them as she went out, "I have a feeling something wonderful is going to happen tonight!"

Mrs Cowart picked up the book she was reading and settled down in her favorite spot in the living room. After a couple of paragraphs her thoughts wandered. Suddenly, she realized she was very unhappy. A strange feeling gripped her, as if she was only flesh and muscle, with no bones and couldn't sit up. A fog bank of emptiness rolled over her. She could hear the TV blaring in the other room, yet she felt completely alone. Peter was watching some "cops and robbers" show. An ambulance wailed on the program and she shivered violently. An accumulation of all the horrible, lost feelings of a lifetime washed over her.

"What is wrong with me?" she asked herself. "Am I sick? Is this some kind of spiritual attack?" Never in her life had anything like this happened to her. She had an incredible urge to run to Mr Cowart and ask him to hold her. "He'll think I'm losing my mind," she said to herself. "Oh, great. Now I'm talking to myself. This is the first step to insanity."

She got into bed with her Bible. But that didn't bring comfort or relief from the feelings that pressed on her like a physical weight. At last she drifted into a fitful sleep.

Ring! Ring! The telephone cut through the silence like a knife. Mrs Cowart sat up. She was wide awake and strained to hear the muffled voice of her husband in the other room.

Crash! The door flew open hitting the wall. "Get up! Quick!" Mr Cowart barked. "Love's been in a wreck and she's hurt, bad." He began frantically throwing on his clothes.

Mrs Cowart leapt out of bed. She felt thoroughly confused. All manner of thoughts crowded her mind. *Should I bother with dressing in a situation like this? What do I wear? Do I put on shoes? Comb my hair?* "Who was on the phone?" she asked. "What happened?"

"It was the security guard at University Hospital. He said come quickly, but not to have a wreck," his voice broke into a sob.

Richard and Mike were just driving up when Mr and Mrs Cowart walked out the door. "Stay here with Peter," their dad ordered, "we'll call you as soon as we know something."

"No way!" Peter was crying. Love was the only one who could handle him. He obeyed her better than either one of his parents. "You can't make me stay!"

Mrs Cowart knew the agony of waiting and wanted all her boys around her. Mr Cowart couldn't stop them from coming anyway. Everyone leapt in the car and began the tortuous twenty-mile trip to the hospital. Mrs Cowart gripped Mike's hand with all her strength as they sped silently down the rough, winding country road.

A deer bounded across their path, but Mr Cowart hardly slowed. Mrs Cowart looked at it in wonder. The deer made an impression on her as if she saw its eyes, calm and assuring.

She was strangely numb, but the thought came to her, "God doesn't make mistakes." She knew it was true and it comforted her.

Mr Cowart began to pray, but she couldn't. She was too numb. Love hated to suffer and was so sensitive to pain. What was she suffering now? What horror was her flesh being subjected to? With every atom in her body, with the very depths of her being, Mrs Cowart wanted to change places with her daughter. She said it to God with all the earnestness she possessed, "Take me, Lord. Let me suffer, not her. Not my beautiful daughter."

Something big broke inside her heart. She felt it crack open. For the first time she felt she truly understood what love meant.

She remembered how Love looked in the white dress. A long-ago memory flooded into her mind with devastating clarity. "I hear him, Mommy. Jesus is calling me to heaven." Love was only six years old when she marched in and announced this to her mother.

Mrs Cowart had been so startled she had pricked her finger as she hemmed Love's dress. She remembered how she had been so careful not to spot the little white eyelet material with her blood. The white dress Love wore tonight would be stained forever.

The hole in her finger had long since healed, but would the hole in her heart ever heal?

In the emergency room they were met by Elaine. Her son, Jay, had been driving the car. Although he was in critical condition too, she was doubly heartsick, feeling his responsibility as the driver.

The Cowarts wrapped their arms around her knowing it could easily have been one of their teenage sons in Jay's place. There were always hazards when teenagers drive. No blame was placed, only shared grief that forged an iron ring of love binding their hearts.

The starkness of the barren little closet that served as a waiting room was softened by the officials' concern and kindness. Minutes crawled like hours. Finally, they learned that Jay would recover. Love's condition, however, was grave.

It had been around eight o'clock when Love left the house, and after nine when the crushing call came. The Cowarts had assumed the kids were long gone, perhaps downtown, when the wreck occurred. But they learned it had been only minutes after they'd left, at the same moment the emptiness engulfed Mrs Cowart. The wailing siren she'd mistaken for one on TV had been speeding to the scene where her daughter lay crushed in twisted metal.

She and Jay had sped down the winding two-lane road. At a place where the road dipped, a deer had run across their path. Jay swerved, losing control of the car as they topped a rise. A wide live oak tree stood just off the road. They hit it head on at around sixty miles per hour. Mrs Cowart wondered if it been the same deer they had seen as they drove in to the hospital.

Waiting in that bare little room, unable to sit, Mr Cowart couldn't seem to control the tremors that wracked his body. He clutched his wife's hand as tears streamed down his weathered face. He was still the strong, cool dad Love had admired so much. But although she had written that he never showed emotion, it now flowed out of him in rivers.

Mrs Cowart felt a physical pain in her chest as though someone was tearing out her heart, yet somewhere deeper, down in her soul, was peace. She knew Love was going to die. But the strange peace washed over her as suddenly as the emptiness had earlier. Over and over the words hammered her mind, "God doesn't make mistakes. No accidents happen to his children."

She could hardly understand it. There was no fighting, no striving. She wasn't wishing this wasn't happening. She felt no disbelief. For the first time she understood what the Bible meant when it promised, "God's peace passes all our understanding."

After about an hour the doctor came in. "Mrs Cowart, you might want to sit down."

"That's not necessary," she replied. She already knew.

At that very hospital fifteen years before the whole family had gathered to welcome Love into the family. "It's a girl!" Mr Cowart had exclaimed.

Together again, the family stood in the same hospital for quite a different reason – to tell her good-bye.

The Prophecy

Nobody spoke on the long drive back to Heathermoor Farm. Everyone walked straight to the place that held her memory the closest, her room. On top of all the mess on her white bed were her Bible and a book, the one they had all seen her carrying constantly over the past week. No one paid attention to it till now.

The cover displayed a painting of clouds with a sunburst beaming behind, radiating through their cracks and along the edges. The title was like the voice of God himself, *Come Away My Beloved.* It was an interpretation of the book in the Bible, Song of Solomon, as a letter from God to his beloved people.

Its title faced the little group. Peter picked it up and found an underlined passage. "My will is not a place but a condition... You can trust me, knowing that any pressure I bring upon thy life is initiated by my love, and I will not do even this unless you're willing ... because you are depending on me for guidance and direction, I shall give it."

He couldn't keep reading, for tears choked his words.

Mrs Cowart picked up where he left off, "Release thy grief. Never bury thy griefs: but offer them up to Me. Thou wilt relieve thy soul of much strain if ye can lay every care in My hand ... Turn it over to Me and in doing so, ye shall free Me to work it out."

Mr Cowart opened Love's Bible. In the very front was a reference written in her flowing writing. Turning to the location, Psalm 27:4, he found the verse starred and underlined. It read, "The only thing I want from God, the thing I seek most of all, is the privilege of meditating in His Temple, living in His presence every day of my life, delighting in His incomparable perfection and glory. There I'll be when troubles come. He will hide me. He will set me on a high rock."

As the family gathered in the living room with friends and neighbors, they felt as if God himself had left them a note. "I called her away, Love, My beloved."

Peter slept in Love's bed that night and never went back to his room. The next morning he pulled out a disorderly stack of papers, her diary. It was written on farm stationery and notebook paper. Randomly he pulled one page from the messy pile.

It was dated July 1.

"To Whoever Cares: Today is July 1, 1973. I have just been revealed something, and it is that I'm going to die young. I'm not sure exactly how I feel about it. Right now I'm crying, but maybe tomorrow I'll be glad. I'm different, very different. I've been aware of this for a long time. I don't fit this world. But I have learned one thing that's made me able to live and that is to love. I can love more deeply than any other thing. It's the most real thing I know. I want to express how I love to you, so you can too.

I love you world – you people. I love you, and I want us all to be happy. I want to show you how before I die. My life is a constant wanting but not getting. I guess it's better than getting and not being thankful. All I know is someday in heaven I'll be fulfilled. Earthly things don't really matter anyway. But I want my life, my death, my words, my love, something of me to change this old world. I hope you can understand the deep meaning behind what I stupidly try to express. Try to understand I'm a lot more than I seem to be. When I die, I want everything natural and normal and nothing hidden or changed. Because my life begins after my death."

"Look at the date." Mrs Cowart pointed. "July 1. John, don't you remember how Love changed in July. She stopped complaining and began being so kind and helpful. I knew something had happened. The thought of heaven purified her heart."

Mr Cowart wrapped his arms around his wife and they cried tears of sorrow, relief and joy. "Thank you, Lord, for giving us a glimpse into heaven."

Two little cousins were with Peter when he discovered the letter. The mystery of it wasn't lost on them. Peter echoed their question to his mother, "Mama, do you think Love was really an angel?"

She rolled her eyes and laughed through tears. "Definitely not."

Love was the only one Peter ever really obeyed. He was devoted to his sister and took her death harder than anyone else. He ran into the woods in anguish later that day. Mrs Cowart worried about him but knew he needed time to grieve. When he returned he was radiant.

"Momma!" he yelled. "If someone gave Love a new car we wouldn't want to take it away from her. Would we?"

"No Peter," Mrs Cowart smiled and hugged him close.

"Heaven's like getting a new car. We wouldn't want to take her away from there would we?"

A new car was the living end in a thirteen year old's mind. Mrs Cowart was comforted that God had given Peter a tangible example for him to relate with heaven.

Earlier that month Love had confided in Franny, "At my funeral I want to have daisies for the flowers. I want everyone to be happy and act normal."

"Shut up Love, you're such a freak!" had been Franny's response. But now she told Mrs Cowart about Love's request.

Daisies at the funeral?

Love, her daughter, so young and full of life?

Her daughter, who had just begun to open up to her.

Her daughter, just beginning to taste life in all its fullness.

The sudden irrevocable end of youth, beauty and joy crushed Mrs Cowart. The pain in the hearts of those left behind, the hole Love left in their family by her death, the nightmare of a breathless, battered body, the desolation of the grave, the tragedy of a life unfulfilled, a budding rose crushed before it reached full bloom. All these thoughts and images rolled over her one after another like waves crashing on the beach.

She felt like the Stallion Rex when he could no longer hold his head high. His life, like Love's, had been cut short. She was tied to him somehow. The very horror and offense of death was wrong. It was totally illogical. It was not what God had planned. It was the result of man rebelling against God, choosing to worship himself and created things rather than the Creator.

The cross of Christ fell like a shadow across her mind. It destroyed death forever. That was the reason Jesus came in the first place – to destroy death and restore our friendship with God. Through his death on the cross he removed the sting of death so that whoever believed in him, even though they die on earth, they will live with him forever in heaven.

This was her hope. She clung to it like a lifeline.

When she looked to Christ, she felt peace. Incredibly, she even felt joy. She knew with certainty she'd see Love again. This would only be a separation. There would be no funeral. Hadn't Love said, "My life begins after my death?" They wouldn't have a funeral; they'd have a praise service.

Mr Cowart later wrote: "It was Saturday, the day Love's Praise Service was to be held. The sun was bright and it was a beautiful morning. We dressed and went to Nita's parents' home to meet the others in the family and drove then to the cemetery for the graveside service.

"No one seemed sad, we were about the business of our Lord and He gave each one of us individually His assurance that all was right.

"As we sat before the flower covered casket, I kept saying to myself, 'She is not here, she is risen to be with the Lord on high. This is what the songs are all about. I know she is in His presence this very second.' I could feel no special care for this casket and its contents; my little girl is risen and borne on angels' wings into heaven.

"After the service, each member of the family picked a daisy from the floral spray on the casket and pinned it to his lapel. We then drove directly to the church and went in as a group. I felt a sense of almost euphoria as I knew what we were doing was God's will. It seemed the clearest and most right thing for us to be doing.

"Frank prayed and then we sang a song, only I couldn't make a sound. I tried to sing; Nita stood next to me and sang out in a beautiful clear, sweet voice. But I couldn't make a sound.

"As we sat back down I began to look about this familiar sanctuary. This is where our children joined the church, where we had attended school programs and Christmas pageants to see our little ones perform. In less than a year Mike would graduate from high school in this place. In another year Richard would graduate. In yet one more year and Love ... but Love wouldn't graduate here. Our hearts would never swell with pride as we watched her join the processional, filled with hopes and dreams and great intentions, to complete this important part of her life.

"Even more, we would never see Love join in marriage to the one she chose to share her life with. And we would never experience the joy of witnessing her children baptized or feel the wonder of Love's children, our grandchildren squirming on our knees during church.

"And suddenly I ached with pain as I contemplated our loss. The congregation was singing again, only I had no song and my eyes burned. I was utterly desolate and blinded with grief. I could hear Nita's sweet clear voice, strong and joyful, and I wondered, 'How can she do it? Doesn't she realize how much we have lost?'

"And then, just as quickly as I had taken my eye off Jesus, I opened them again and saw things aright. We haven't lost

Love; we have given her to the Lord. Men might say we had no choice in the matter, but our not holding on, our act of accepting His will and gladly committing her to Him was our act of obedience. Yes Lord, we gladly give her life to You, and our own as well, if You desire.

"It is altogether right that Nita should be singing to the Lord for this is Love's wedding celebration, and she has been joined in marriage to the King!

"How much like the disciple Peter I am, for while I kept my eyes on Jesus I had walked where no man had walked before. And the instant I looked down, the minute I surveyed my situation through the eyes of man, I began to sink. But as with Peter, Jesus held out His hand to me and lifted me to safety. Only when I forget the lesson, only when I lapse back into self pity and indulge myself with the human approach to heavenly things do I begin to sink. The lesson is so very clear – keep your eyes upon Jesus, look full into His wonderful face, and the joys of this world go strangely dim in the light of His wonder and grace."

Phantom Rider

*L*ove's death affected many lives. Mrs Cowart told us about several teenagers who had written or called saying they'd invited Christ into their lives after Love's death. They wanted an intimate relationship with God like Love had. Mrs Cowart wrote her story and it has been photocopied and passed from hand to hand until it has reached many people around the globe.

Katy and I had longed to be like Love so much that when we were only ten we each wrote, "God has revealed to me I'm going to die young. I want everyone to be happy and not sad because I'm going to be with Jesus."

Every time I got hurt I thought, *this is it; I'm going to die, just like Love.* At times I wished I would die.

March 5th finally rolled around. My mother took me to the DMV first thing and we waited as they unlocked the door. I was ready for my driver's license and so was she.

I passed with flying colors. After all I'd been driving since I was ten.

My license was liberation for both of us. Mom handed me the car keys and swore she'd never make that drive to the barn again, "As long as I live."

I spent every spare moment at the barn, even getting P.E. credit for working the horses. Katy and I helped train more and more horses, just like Love and Franny had.

Mr Cowart, standing in the center of the ring, would shout, "Take up a little more snaffle rein. Raise his head!"

From the other side Mrs Cowart would call, "Loosen the snaffle and take in more curb rein, his nose is sticking out!" By the time I trotted on around to Mr Cowart again he'd yell, "Don't take up so much curb rein, his nose was fine!" To which Mrs Cowart would yell something else contradictory as I passed her on the other side. I guess that's the way of it with two chiefs.

I broke and trained a little black pony named Velvet. I halter-trained her when she was a year old. Velvet was not a true black pony; she had a tiny bit of white on her back left fetlock. "A white sock," we'd say.

I loved Velvet and spent hours lunging her. "Walk. Good girl, Velvet. Okay, trot." Snapping the long whip as I said, "Trot," Velvet got the message and began to trot. After trotting in circles for a minute or two I'd call, "Walk," and jerk the lunge line. She'd slow down.

After going through this exercise every day for weeks I could command her with my voice to walk, trot, canter, whoa, and do it all again. She followed me like a dog. When I stopped, she'd stop. When I walked, she'd follow.

Finally, the day came to mount her. I had trained her, so it was my privilege to be the first to ride her. Mrs Cowart called, "Oh, Mary, she looks so beautiful. You have the best hands of any rider out here."

Wow! I thought, the best seat *and* the best hands. I puffed my chest out and held my hands steady. Velvet trotted evenly up and back in front of the barn, then unaccountably bolted.

Velvet got spooked by something or other and – oh my – I was so busy concentrating on my good seat and good hands that I tumbled off backward. She bucked, kicking like a real rodeo bronco. Then that tiny pony bolted straight to the five-foot fence and threw herself over it as if she was in the steeplechase. Her belly scraped the top and the stirrups clanged on the wood. She went wild in the pasture, running and bucking. I was glad I fell early because clearly she had a bee in her bonnet about something.

Velvet and I finally came to an understanding – she'd let me ride her and Mr Cowart wouldn't horsewhip her. She never went berserk again, but she kept me on my toes. She graduated to the double bridle and I worked her while Mrs Cowart coached me. One afternoon she said, "The

Hueytown horse show is coming up, I think you've got Velvet ready. Let's try her out."

The next afternoon I came out to the barn and went straight to Velvet's stall. She wasn't there. I wondered if they anticipated me coming and were preparing her for me. Walking into the hallway I saw no horse standing in the crossties. The fans hummed and one of the horses nickered. I rubbed my hand on his soft nose as I passed by and headed out the back of the barn. There in the large ring was Velvet. I couldn't believe it. Jane was riding her and Mr Cowart stood in the center of the ring calling out directions.

I didn't know if I should stay in the hallway and pretend I didn't see, or go into the ring and watch. Deciding on the latter, I arrived just in time to hear Mr Cowart praising Jane. "I think you should show her at Hueytown this weekend."

It felt as if he'd punched me in the stomach. Hot tears pricked my eyes and I couldn't breathe. I turned around so they wouldn't see me cry and race-walked back to the barn.

Jane ride Velvet? I had trained her. Why was Mr Cowart doing this to me? Velvet was my horse. Well, she did belong to the Cowarts, but I had worked with her for a whole year. It wasn't fair! I lived for horse shows. There was nothing I loved more than performing before a crowd.

More and more he let Katy ride the best horses. I was given the leftover, loser horses to work. My pride was wounded. I felt rejected by the man I loved like a second father. *I'm the one with the good hands! Didn't you hear Mrs Cowart?* I wanted to shout.

Arriving at the barn one afternoon I walked in to see Mr Cowart and Katy deep in conversation. They readied one of the show horses for her to work. I felt like a phantom. Neither took notice of me.

The horse clopped out of the barn led by Mr Cowart. He held the horse still for Katy to mount. She grabbed the saddle and put her foot in the stirrup. The horse was a giant and she struggled a bit.

I scoffed to myself. I wouldn't struggle. He should let me ride.

Once up, she trotted to the ring with Mr Cowart following, calling out instructions. Neither one acknowledged my presence.

I slithered out to the pasture, threw myself down in the tall grass and stared at the sky. Tears slipped out of the side of my eyes and rolled into my ears. I couldn't understand what had happened. I thought I was the top rider, the Cowart's darling. Now I didn't exist.

"God, why don't you take me like you did Love?" I choked on my tears. "Don't you love me as much as you loved her? If I die, then they'll all be sorry they treated me so badly."

The words to a popular Police song on the radio echoed in my thoughts, "And you'll be sorry when I'm dead and all this guilt will be on your head."

I lay still, exhausted from crying, and closed my eyes. Everything was quiet. I felt the earth rotate on its axis. I wished it would stop so I'd fly out into space. One of the horses came up and snuffled me to see if I was edible.

A thought whispered in my mind.,"Die to yourself."

Do what?

"Die to yourself. Die to your desire to be first. Die to your desire to be recognized. Die to your desire to be served. I don't want you to die physically, I just want you to die to your selfishness."

"I'm not selfish!" I said aloud. But I knew that wasn't true. I knew it down deep, that's why I was so upset. I was mad because everybody didn't bow down to me, "Oh, great rider. Mary the marvelous!"

"It would be so much easier just to die," I moaned.

"Yes, but that's not what I have for you. If you want to be first, you must be last. If you want to be great, you must serve." Verses in the Bible I had read the night before poured into my mind.

I sat up on my elbows and watched Katy finish the workout. In that moment I made a clutch decision. Instead of going in the barn and asking if I could work the next horse, I'd go ask if I could wash Katy's horse and walk him for the cool down. I'd brush and prepare horses for others. I'd not ask to ride. I'd wait for Mr Cowart to ask me.

"No way!" I gritted my teeth. I didn't want to leave my party. It was my pity party and I wasn't ready to give it up.

That's when they attacked.

Red ants, fire ants, piss ants are names Southerners had awarded the little creatures that live to torment. They're called red ants because they're red, fire ants because they burn like fire when they bite, and piss ants — well you get the idea. They lived in colonies where they trained like soldiers.

There must be a captain who went out and gave the order, "Climb up that leg men! Go quietly. Don't disturb a hair. Nobody bite till I give the order." When all the little ants covered both legs the captain gave the order, "Now men, for queen and country!" Then the ants all bit at the same time leaving tiny white blisters that itched for days.

"Okay! Okay! I'm going."

I jumped up, slapping my legs and swallowing my pride to become the servant of all.

A few days later I heard Mr Cowart marveling, "Mary's really different. What happened?"

New girls came to the barn. They thought of Katy and I like we had thought of Love and Franny.

Kari, Jennifer and Emily began to follow us around like puppies. I hadn't the coolness of Franny and was irritated, wanting to leave them behind.

By that time we had lost our fear of the woods at night and camped often. Midnight rides became ho-hum, almost.

When the little girls camped with us the first time we got very little sleep.

Emily shrieked at least every fifteen minutes, "What's that!"

Nancy got so tired of this that she threatened to throw her in the river if she screamed again.

Kari ended up hiking up to the house where she slept in the girls' room upstairs.

Next morning she asked Mrs Cowart the question that remains a Cowart family treasure. "Mrs Cowart, will I ever have a Mr Cowart." We all loved and admired Mr Cowart. However, Kari did get her wish, literally. When she grew up Richard asked her to marry him. Ah, me. At least one of us girls got a Cowart boy.

The little girls grew up, continuing the traditions passed down by Love and Franny. Each one became a new child in the Cowart family. Love was taken, but in her place were many other girls who loved the Cowarts as dearly, or more dearly than their own parents.

Each has their own story that could fill more pages than I could ever write. Jennifer and Courtney lit up the woods one night while camping at Camp Lumberjack. Jennifer, a budding pyromaniac, liked to watch the flames shoot up in the sky as she squirted lighter fluid on the fire. Sirens shattered the night as the local fire brigade drove their trucks through the pasture to put out the flames that leapt in the treetops.

At another camp out, Jennifer and Courtney, always wanting to be helpful, went to the barn that night and took apart all the tack to clean it. Next morning when the Cowarts came to the barn they found two girls asleep on heaps of dismantled bridles and saddles.

Who knew those two would grow up and take over Heathermoor from the Cowarts one day?

Holidays are awful times when you've lost a loved one. They magnify the loss because that is when all the family comes together. Christmas is especially hard. One less Christmas gift lies under the tree. One less stocking hangs from the mantle.

The Cowarts' presents only multiplied as the girls at the barn wanted to give them gifts. Mrs Cowart painted portraits of each girl's horse and wrapped it in shiny Christmas paper. They hosted festive parties where we sang carols and exchanged presents.

Diving into their hall closet, we borrowed winter jackets to go catch the ponies and ride under the winter stars hoping to catch the animals kneeling on Christmas Eve to worship the babe in the manger. I never knew if she caught them at it, but I hoped I would.

College came for me and I did take a horse with me, Christopher Robin, a two year old. However, I never rode him across Auburn's campus, like Mrs Cowart had when she was a coed.

Tragedy dogged the Cowarts. A few years after I had left for college Mr Oden decided to cash in his investment. The Cowarts didn't have the money to buy the farm and were turned out with hundreds of horses and nowhere to go. Over the next several years they went from farm to farm with their herd of horses and girls like Bedouins.

One day as Mr Cowart helped a rider mount, God unexpectedly called him home. He joined Love, leaving Mrs Cowart alone.

But she still has a gaggle of girls who love and surround her. She paints beautiful portraits of horses and animals and still teaches us of God's love through his creation.

On early mornings when the fog still clings to the hollows between the mountains, you may see her lunging a filly. She still breeds and raises Saddlebreds. If you wake early and drive down Highway 119, look for her.

Epilogue

After living in Oregon for fifteen years, I returned to the place of my youth.

Heathermoor Farm had been subdivided into four smaller farms.

My old riding instructor, Jeannie Cox, kept hunter jumpers in the old barn.

When I visited she told me a strange story.

"Every now and then, in the middle of the night we see a girl in a white dress, riding across the field on a brown horse. It scared the family on the hill so much they called their priest. He came out to the farm and said, 'The people who lived here have moved on. They are no longer here.' That night-time visitor vanished for a while. But she's been back. Every now and then we hear her still."

Is Love the mysterious phantom girl? Does she ride horses in heaven? Does Love ride Madame down to her childhood home, looking for the girls who followed in her footsteps, for her family, torn from their home

219

they so loved? Or is the vision just an echo? Does the land replay a sweet memory? Does it press rewind and watch its favorite child again and again?

The Bible says to be absent from the body is to be present with the Lord, and I know Love is with the Lord. As Peter said, "How could we wish her back from such a wonderful place?"

It's not her.

What about you?

Do you know where you would go if you were to die today? You will die one day. Call upon Jesus. Ask him to be your Savior and Lord. Then you can know God personally just like Love.

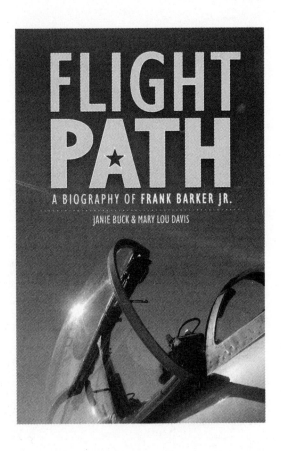

'The story of Frank Barker is an amazing account of how God uses the faithful and the humble. In a marvelous way Christ sought him, saved him, and made him an effective instrument for the building up of the church. What a remarkable and encouraging legacy!'

John MacArthur, Grace Community Church, Los Angeles, California

ISBN: 978-185792-918-8